ELVIS, JESUS AND COCA-COLA

Kinky Friedman, former leader of the band The Texas Jewboys, lives on a ranch in the Texas Hill Country with two dogs, two cats and one armadillo. He is the author of eight internationally acclaimed mystery novels and six country music albums.

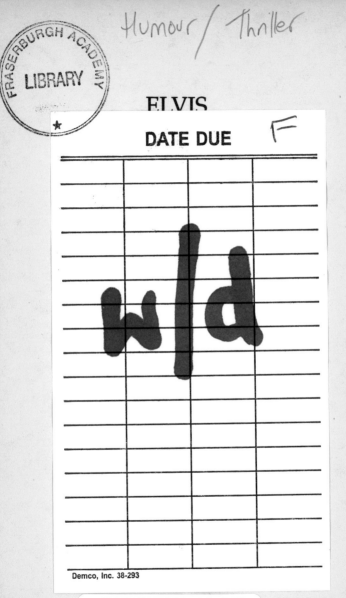

DATE DUE

First published in Great Britain in 1993
in *More Kinky Friedman*
by Faber and Faber Limited
3 Queen Square London WC1N 3AU
Open market paperback edition first published in 1993
This paperback edition first published in 1994

Printed in England by Clays Ltd, St Ives plc

A CIP record for this book is
available from the British Library

ISBN 0-571-17192-3

4 6 8 10 9 7 5

1

At Tom Baker's wake, quite well attended, as the wakes and funerals of misunderstood people usually are, I sang 'Ride 'em Jewboy.' The song is a western translation of what is essentially an eastern experience, the holocaust. It is not surprising that this song had been a favorite of Baker's. As Brendan Behan said: 'The Irish and the Jews do not share a nation; they share a psychosis.'

Goat Carson recited a poem he'd written for the Bakerman, the last two lines of which I remember: 'Between the gutter and the stars/People are what people are . . .'

Tom Baker was.

I first met the Bakerman on the gang plank of Noah's Ark. The last time I saw him, the lifespan of a sea tortoise later, was from the frosty window of a hack at four o'clock in the morning out in front of the old Lone Star Cafe in New York. It's not there anymore, the Lone Star. The neighborhood needed another Bennigan's. New York's still there, of course, in a manner of speaking. At least it still exists in the recently colorized imagination of terminally ill children. And who of us isn't one of them?

The Lone Star was heavily shuttered, the Bakerman was heavily monstered, standing on the curbside wearing old trousers, a long gray woolen coat from some forgotten war, a blue knit cap, and an intransigently Irish expression halfway down a country road between happiness and despair. I remember snowflakes dreideling down all around him like slow motion tears from a burned-out guardian angel.

Baker had been one big, tough, talented charming crazy, green-eyed Irishman who men respected and women

1

invariably loved. He was an actor but, because Hollywood was Hollywood and the Bakerman was the Bakerman, most of his more memorable performances were offstage and off-screen. He was a star who only really had the chance to shine into the lives of those who knew him.

Life and death are not without their little ironies and one of them was that Tom Baker died on stage. It was a small stage. It was in the loft of his close friend Bob Brady, an acting coach. Officially, it was called an overdose, but this doesn't tell us much because sooner or later everybody suffers from an overdose. Too many over-the-counter dreams. Too much Early Times. Too many Sunday nights in Los Angeles.

I met Tom Baker's dad for the first time at the wake and noticed in him many of the gestures, mannerisms and voice inflections that you take for granted until you have a dead friend. Tom's father mentioned a film that his son had been working on at the time of his death. I knew about it. Tom had spent a great deal of time and effort on the project. Tom Baker, Movie-maker, he'd called himself. Tom Baker, Trouble-maker, others called him.

The film was a documentary on Elvis impersonators. And, according to Tom's father the film, along with Tom, of course, was missing.

'Do you think you could help us find it?' he asked. 'Our Tom was very proud of it.'

'No prob,' I said confidently. 'Most likely it's just been misplaced. I'll run it down for you in the next day or so.'

I shook his big, sad hand and felt the Bakerman slipping away.

I'd find the film, all right. It couldn't be that difficult, I thought. It had to be somewhere between the gutter and the stars.

2

There is a period of time after the death of someone very close to you when everyone you meet appears to be a nerd. You can't understand why elderly women would take the time to knit them sweaters. Quite possibly it is that there have always been a high proportion of nerds in the world and that it requires the cauterization of someone with sparkle to highlight the tedium of almost everyone else.

'At least all cats are pretty hip,' I said to the cat. 'My beautiful little pet.'

'It's not your pet,' said Ratso from the couch. 'It's your animal companion.' Ratso was my sometime Dr Watson and oft-time housepest. When he wasn't busy getting up my sleeve, he was the editor of *National Lampoon*.

I thought about it for a moment as I lit a cigar with a kitchen match, always keeping the end of the cigar just above the level of the flame. I didn't answer Ratso or really take notice of him. Neither did the cat.

'Pet is a demeaning word. Animal companion,' he repeated. 'That's the correct way of stating it.'

'*You're* my animal companion,' I said.

It had been several days since Tom Baker's wake and Ratso had been logging considerable time at my humble loft on Vandam Street. His claim was that the plumbing in his apartment building was being worked on but ever so often I thought I caught him glancing at me with pity in his eyes. Maybe I was just getting paranoid like everyone else in New York, but it crossed my desk several times that he knew how close I'd been to the Bakerman and maybe he was here on some skewered kind of suicide watch like you read about in the *National Enquirer*. On the other hand, the plumbing in Ratso's apartment left a lot to be desired.

At last, I could no longer take Ratso's eyes following my movements around the living room. The more he watched me like a giant hood-eyed tropical bird, the more nervous I became and the more intense became my pacing back and forth across the loft. The cat, as a kitten, had been fascinated by this pacing and used to follow back and forth in my footsteps. As she grew older she tired of this ridiculous activity but still seemed to enjoy watching me pace much in the manner of a slightly bored British matron watching a badminton match. Now that the cat was reaching *The Prime of Miss Jean Brodie*, she could care less whether or not I got a pogo stick and jumped through my asshole for America.

The cat, of course, had never particularly liked Ratso. I didn't know if this was instinct, anti-Semitism, or merely feline malice. I wasn't sure I wanted to know.

'Ratso,' I said, after several more hours had ticked by, 'are you here because I have a broken heart or because you have a broken dumper?'

'Either would seem a compelling reason,' said Ratso. 'Why do you wish to know?'

'Because if you're worried about me hanging myself from a shower rod, I'm going to get a forklift in here and get you the hell out of here. *Then* I'll hang myself from a shower rod.'

'Sounds sensible,' Ratso said.

We bantered on in this fashion for an interminable length of time, whereupon Ratso finally took his leave. He said he had to check his plumbing but I could tell he was going out in a snit. I also observed that he left a large valise containing the viaticum of his life behind the sofa. Like a clockwork MacArthur, I knew someday he'd return.

I appreciated Ratso's concern but I needed to be alone. For one thing, I'd already checked with Bob Brady, Baker's close friend, who'd scoured the loft where Tom had lived and not found a trace of his final cinematic effort. One of Tom's assistants on the film, a guy named Legs, had already reported to Baker's father that the film was missing from the lab. If the film wasn't in the loft and wasn't in the lab that meant I only had to look everywhere else.

Later, in the week following the Bakerman's wake, I reoccupied my old base camp in the foothills of Mt Depression. I stayed in the loft like Emily Dickinson, smoking cigars, drinking coffee, periodically feeding the cat, and occasionally feeding myself some warmed-over detritus from the back of the refrigerator, the dates on both of our cartons seemingly having expired.

I did observe a minor behavioral change on my part during that time. I'd taken to farting loudly, ostentatiously and, I felt, rather humorously, on the increasingly rare occasions when friends of mine, including Ratso, came by the loft. I don't know why I did this.

Maybe it was a cry for help.

3

It was at this time that I began seeing some rather uncanny parallels between my life and the life of Jesus. Both of us, of course, were of the Jewish persuasion. Neither of us ever really had a home to speak of. Neither of us ever married during the course of our lives. Neither of us ever actually held a job during the course of our lives. We both just basically traveled around the countryside irritating people.

'Maybe Jesus can help us,' I said to the cat. 'Maybe He can find the missing film about Elvis impersonators.'

The cat looked at me as if I were clinically ill, but she stood her ground beside me on the desk. Thus encouraged, I continued.

'Maybe Jesus can help me run down this Legs character. I've left three messages on his answering machine but he's not responding to therapy.'

The cat looked at me as one stares at a place where a rainbow has recently been.

'Stop looking at me with pity in your eyes,' I said, as I attempted to brush her off the desk. She moved down a bit just out of my reach and continued to stare at me.

'Let us pray,' I said to the cat. We both bowed our heads.

'Dear God, Jesus, Buddha, or L. Ron Hubbard, please help us find this documentary about Elvis impersonators. We trust the Bakerman and Elvis are with you now and should vouch for the sincerity of our efforts. We know you will enjoy the company of the Bakerman. Elvis, of course, during his entire career never played to an empty seat. Towards the end, unfortunately, he became somewhat of a chemical puppet and had to have his rather protuberant stomach wound extensively with saran wrap prior to going on stage, but Christ, you know how it is with idols.

'As I look at what's going on in the world I can see that you guys have been very busy watching every sparrow – '

Here I winked at the cat.

' – nonetheless, we'd appreciate hearing from you soon.'

The cat blinked both eyes rather doubtfully and looked at the ceiling.

I didn't really expect to hear from L. Ron Hubbard. And Buddha hadn't spoken to anybody in years. But I did hope that God or Jesus might be more forthcoming. They'd been almost garrulous in recent times, speaking to psychics, football coaches, political candidates, and Oral Roberts to name only a few. I was quite hopeful.

I made an espresso, puffed on a cigar and encouraged the cat to be patient. I took the espresso over to the kitchen window sill where the cat joined me. We waited. I did not bring an ashtray. The world was my ashtray.

Two espressos and half a cigar later there had been no sign from the heavens. The view from the kitchen window was pretty ho-hum. A riot of gray. God and Jesus, apparently, were not saying dick. Either they didn't exist, they didn't care, or they were both autistic.

'The power of prayer,' I said to the cat.

I picked up a *Daily News* and, somewhat desultorily, turned a few pages looking for my pal McGovern's by-line. It would've been heartening to see something like: 'Kinky, your little friends are wrong.' But there was nothing.

Well, almost nothing. *The Daily News* had occasionally taken to giving McGovern the 'People Page,' thereby making him the only super-intelligent, six foot five inch, two hundred and forty pound Irish society editor in the world. In today's column McGovern pointed out that for the past decade, developers and pollution had threatened Henry David Thoreau's Walden Pond, and that over the years various groups had been fighting to keep the pond pristine and primitive as it had been in Thoreau's time. Of course, there were others inexorably moving toward making the pond look like New Jersey. Both groups were distasteful in their own way and, I reflected, as I lit a fresh cigar, so was McGovern. I didn't think too highly of vapid pop stars who pirouetted up from their sound stages and multi-track studios to embrace global causes. But global causes needed all the help they could get. Just because Michael Jackson was the proud owner of the skeletal remains of the Elephant Man, was no reason for me to cast asparagus on these nerds trying to save Walden Pond.

The developers, of course, were the bad guys, but at least in a somewhat perverted way, they were honest. All they wanted was a lot of money so they could buy a big hairy steak, a trophy wife, a boat, and time to kill a few bambis on the way to Belize. Developers, in fact, sounded rather dangerously like normal Americans. Rock stars saving the world could be equally tedious. McGovern appeared to agree with me for at the bottom of the page he ran a large glitzy photo of a group of celebrities dressed to the hilt in chic, Hollywood drag at a cocktail party to save Walden Pond. Under the photo McGovern ran a quote from Thoreau: 'Beware any enterprise that requires new clothes.'

I looked out the window again and at last I saw a vision. It was not clear if the vision was biblical or not, but I certainly hoped she was. Time would tell. A gorgeous blonde about nine foot tall in some kind of endangered species coat was crossing Vandam toward my loft. She appeared to be walking two little pet squirrels on leashes. Or maybe they were her animal companions. One thing was for sure, they were the luckiest squirrels in New York.

She looked up for a moment and I saw her face. That was a vision, too. She did not have that humorless, cold, brittle, Teutonic look. She appeared vibrant, full of fun, adorable – and it's hard for tall women to appear adorable. She looked very sophisticated and, at the same time, like someone you might've left at the county fair of your dreams. Someone that should've always been with you.

I watched her till she walked out of sight. Then I watched the fire escape, the exposed brick walls of the warehouse down the street, a dollop of gray sky, a limo, a slow-motion man going through a garbage can in the world of the dimly lit. My fellow Americans, I thought, rolling around in the ancient streets like dung-beetles grimly pursuing happiness as they're being run down by life.

I smoked the cigar. I stroked the cat. Then I closed my eyes and looked out over Walden Pond.

4

Sometimes life jumps up and bites you in the ass. Like the joke: 'What has four legs and an arm?' The answer: 'Pit bull.' Very few people find that joke humorous. Even fewer find life humorous, but maybe that's part of the problem.

For me, at the moment, life was about as funny as Clint Eastwood's monkey. Not only was I suffering the loss of a man whom I was belatedly realizing to have been my best friend, but I was rapidly coming to the conclusion that when I did finally locate his assistant, Legs, I was going to have his broken. My lonely, hermetic, disenfranchised Emily Dickinson mood was turning positively Kafkaesque. I needed some fun in my life whether I wanted it or not.

I was sitting at my desk in the loft one cold stormy afternoon trying to decide whether to kill myself or go bowling when the phones rang. I let 'em have their head for a while. Didn't want anybody to think I was lonely or hungry or looking for work. Hell, I might be busy as a bee for the rest of my life looking for this Elvis impersonator documentary. I didn't mind hearing the phones ring a bit. It meant somebody somewhere wanted me. You take your comfort where you can.

My phone set up was about as interesting as collecting chinch bugs in Uganda, but it was all I had going at the

9

moment. Two red phones on my desk, one for each half of my brain, were both connected to the same line. There was little practical value to this but when they rang together, which they always did, it made you feel like somebody. I had a slightly effeminate pink pastel princess phone in the bedroom which lately had interrupted me only during the rare occasions of sleep or sexual intercourse. Some day when I'd made a million bucks I planned on getting a phone in the dumper.

I picked up the blower on the left.

'Start talkin',' I said.

'Hi, baby. Do you know who this is?'

I hated it when this happened because most friendly familiar women out of the distant past seemed to sound rather similar to me. I was always caught between being rather surly or going on an extremely unpleasant fishing expedition.

'Can you give me a multiple choice?' I said.

'No,' said the voice.

'Well, let me see,' I said. 'A. Eleanor Roosevelt. B. Squeaky Fromme. C. Mama Cass – '

'Kinkster, you *know* who this is.'

I did.

It was Downtown Judy. She just didn't know she was Downtown Judy because she didn't know there was an Uptown Judy. Both of them thought they were just Judy and that was the way I wanted to keep it. They'd both come into my life, along with a number of others who weren't named Judy, some years ago at about the same time. It was also a time when I was usually so high I'd needed a stepladder to scratch my ass. Neither Judy had been quite the answer, so an elaborate juggling system had evolved, providing for rather exciting near-misses that, on several occasions, brought me fairly close to becoming a castrato in the Vienna Boys Christmas Choir. Keeping the two Judys in ignorance of each other kept me busy and, as an added benefit, kept me in ignorance of joint checking accounts, vacuum cleaners, and booster chairs in family-oriented restaurants. Now was the time, I thought, for the two Judys to make a reentry into my life. I hadn't really spent time with either of them for a while.

By the time I'd hung up the blower it'd been arranged for Downtown Judy to come over to the loft that evening for a little slumber party. Downtown Judy had been a pretty fair actress at one time. Now she was a pretty fair social worker. Her goal, as I understood it, was to use her second career to try to uplift all the people she'd had to step on in her first one. Tonight I was hoping she'd uplift Mister Pinky.

Blower traffic was light that afternoon; I was receiving almost no incoming wounded. As the day grew darker and stormier I seemed to become increasingly disenfranchised from both the rat race and the human race, and began experiencing an inability to differentiate between the two. A possible index of my extreme loneliness was that, after no small degree of personal turmoil, I picked up the blower on the left and called Ratso at his office.

'*National Lampoon,*' said a female voice.

'May I speak to Ratso, please?'

'May I tell him who's calling, please?'

'Gerald McBoing-Boing.'

'May I tell him who you're *with*, sir?' said the secretary, with just the slight flutterings of irritation.

'The Butthead Group.'

'May I tell him what this is in regard to?' she said curtly.

'You can tell him that it's in regard to the little-known fact that many centuries ago Tahitian sailors were believed to have made their way to the Hawaiian Islands in rudimentary canoes, and these noble, primitive men, as they crossed thousands of miles of uncharted, often starless seas, in order to detect ever-so-subtle ocean currents, were said to have, on occasion, placed their scrotums on the wooden floors of their canoes for navigational purposes.'

'Did you call last week?'

She put me on hold.

It wasn't the first time this had happened in the brief, torturous pilgrimage of my life and I doubted if it'd be my last. But holding for Ratso invariably tended to give me pause. Which, if you stop to think about it, is a good thing to have if you're on hold.

'Kinkstah!' Ratso finally said. 'Kinkstah! The Rangers are playin' the Bruins tonight! Got two tickets from J.D.'

J.D. was John Davidson, great former Ranger goalie and friend of mine and Ratso's who'd done a very rare thing – beautifully transitioned from star player to star television commentator. In hockey that doesn't happen often. Of course, not all of the players speak English.

I told Ratso that I had some scoring of my own to do that evening and he took the news good-naturedly, warning me against high-sticking and circus accidents.

'It's gonna be a great game,' Ratso tried one more time. 'You're gonna be sorry you missed it.'

'I'm sure I will,' I said. I had no idea at the time how true were those words. I was just grateful Ratso'd gotten his plumbing fixed.

Sometime later, during the empty walk-in closet of eternity that often passes for dusk in New York, the phones rang in the loft. This time it was the call I'd been waiting for. It was Legs.

'Look, man, I've got something important to talk to you about, but I've got to run.' No pun intended apparently.

'Fine,' I said. 'When can I meet you?'

'Tomorrow afternoon at three. The Monkey's Paw.'

'I know the place.' I'd fried half of my brain cells out in the men's room there, I ought to know the place.

'Ciao,' he said, and was gone.

I cradled the blower.

'Ciao,' I said to the cat.

The cat looked at me questioningly. I blew a nice trail of cigar smoke up at the ceiling.

'Rhymes with meow,' I said.

5

From the kitchen window I could see Downtown Judy coming up Vandam Street like a red tide at sunset. Somewhere in the world there was a sunset. In New York, where there was often no sun or sky to speak of, garish shadows fell like elderly people onto the sidewalks and the dull gray blanket turned darker and bone-chillingly colder, and underneath it the rats and people scurried around faster and faster.

Judy waved up at me from the sidewalk. I opened the window just enough to toss down the little Negro puppet head with the key to the building wedged in its mouth. Ratso had once stumbled across a basket of little Negro puppet heads at a flea market on Canal Street and managed to christian down some guy in a turban for the whole lot. In his enormous generosity he'd given me one and I'd developed a rather close rapport with it. What Ratso had done with all the others only Allah or Uncle Remus knew and neither seemed to be talking.

The puppet head, more durable than most human heads, had already burned through any number of brightly-coloured parachutes and was currently sporting a product

I sold at my shows, the 'Honor America Bandanna', otherwise known as 'the Kinky snot rag'. It was an American flag with fifty stars of David, a picture of the Kinkster, and the slogan: 'Sold American.' As a song, 'Sold American' had been in the top ten on the country charts in 1973. That same year it had been number one in Cadillac, Michigan. As a slogan for a parachute, 'Sold American' shot by the junkies on the sidewalk of normal society a little too rapidly to mean a hell of a lot. Unfortunately, it was the story of many of our lives. But at the moment that didn't mean dick to a tree or to me. My main concern was closing the window before my nose hairs turned to stalactites.

With parachute and puppet head in hand, Downtown Judy opened the large metal door to the building and began the laborious climb to my fourth floor loft. I began the rather laborious task of deciding where to take her for dinner. I wished I could say I loved her. I wished I could say I loved anyone. The way I loved the cat and the Bakerman. Historically, I thought, cats and dead people had always been cheap dates. Easy to love. Easy to keep in your heart.

I took Downtown Judy to the Monkey's Paw. I ate five Jack Daniels and several Dr Peckers on the side as well as about half of a shepherd's pie. Everybody in the place looked vaguely familiar, especially after the third shot. Downtown Judy ate the other half of the pie, along with some kind of Chateau de Cat Piss and we both celebrated the occasion with a small aluminum foil package of new improved Tide that she'd purchased from a nervous pale little man called the Weasel who didn't know he was called the Weasel, just like Downtown Judy didn't know she was Downtown Judy. I reflected, as I killed the fourth shot, how few of us in this crazy world actually know who or what we are. Maybe I was an impeccably dressed, uptight, corporate kind of guy trapped in the shell of a country singer turned amateur detective. Maybe I was an escargot.

I was in relatively high spirits and pretty well walking on my knuckles by the time we got back to the loft. I'd down-shifted to Jameson's Irish Whiskey which I was drinking from my old bull's horn. Between the unpredictable jabbing pain of the Bakerman's death and the quite predictable teeth-grinding effect of the Weasel's product, there were moments when I felt almost human.

Winnie Katz's lesbian dance class in the loft above seemed to have suddenly kicked into high gear. Downtown Judy had kicked off her shoes and stockings and various other extraneous paraphernalia, and the cat, who very much preferred Downtown Judy to Ratso, was purring quietly on the kitchen counter. What more could a man want?

'You know,' I said, as Judy unbuttoned her blouse, 'that I've been impotent now for about twenty-five years.'

'Well, that'll work out fine because I'm afraid this just happens to be that time of the month.'

'You're fuckin' kiddin',' I said.

'I'm not fuckin' kiddin',' said Judy. 'I'm not fuckin' at all.'

The cat and I both looked at Judy. Winnie's dance class continued unabated somewhere in the sky. I killed a subdued shot of Jameson's.

'We could cuddle,' she said.

It was later that night when the phones began to ring rather ominously. I uncuddled myself from Downtown Judy and got out of bed noticing that my Borneo sarong had ridden up to my armpits and quite possibly would've choked me to death if not for the sudden fortuitous circumstances of cuddlaribus interruptus. Some mildly foreboding, unkenable instinct warned me that this was a call that ought to be taken at the desk. Walking on tiptoes (a spiritually transferred trait from my friend John Morgan who'd always walked that way), I made it to the desk by Jewish radar and collared the blower on the right.

It was Sergeant Mort Cooperman, a homicide dick that I'd had some rather extensive and often fairly repellent social intercourse with. Unpleasantries were exchanged. Eventually, he got to the point.

'You know a skirt named Judy?' he asked. The tone and texture of his voice would've jump-started Lauren Bacall.

'Yeah,' I said cautiously, as I made an effort to peer through the gloom into the bedroom. Everything was still.

'Known her long?'

'I've known her for a while,' I said with a hint of irritation. Something was suspish.

'You been in contact with her lately?'

'Yeah,' I said. 'I was in contact with her when you called. Now I think she's adjusting her French Maid costume.'

There was a long, somehow menacing silence on the other end of the line. I glanced nervously into the bedroom again. Judy was still asleep.

When Cooperman spoke again he was giving me an address. It sounded familiar. It was an uptown address.

'Better get over here now,' said Cooperman. 'Otherwise, I may have to book you for necrophilia.'

6

The ride uptown in the hack was uneventful except for a minor altercation between myself and the driver whose appearance and brusque behavior clearly indicated that he came from a country that began with an 'I'. He felt that smoking regulations should be strictly enforced. I felt that, under the circumstances, a little slack might be acceptable. Unfortunately, I wasn't quite sure myself what the circumstances were.

Several potholes and a few near misses served to awaken me a bit from my fairly brain-dead state. Obviously, Cooperman's call had been in regard to Uptown Judy. Remembering how she used to carry a hand gun in her purse, and how occasionally she seemed to be cookin' on another planet, either she'd offed somebody or somebody'd offed her, and neither would've really surprised me. Of course, very little that occurred in New York surprised anybody these days except maybe finding a parking place.

I didn't have a car.

I sincerely hoped nothing had happened to Judy. The last I'd really spoken to her had been months ago. I'd seen her at the Bakerman's wake but she hadn't talked to me. That was strange now that I thought of it. Maybe she'd thought she was giving me my space but I didn't really want my space. I'd been parked in a spiritual towaway zone for years and I wasn't going to start feeding the meter now.

The other thing that was peculiar about all this was why Cooperman was calling me. I'd had fairly peripheral involvement with Uptown Judy, and I didn't really know much about her life. I wasn't exactly her significant other or her next of kin. I hoped to hell she was okay and I'd help her if I could but I was on my way now to meet a homicide dick. I caught a glimpse of the driver's flat, curry-colored eyes glaring at me, shifting with evil intent like the sands of distant dunes.

'Why me, Allah?' I said.

The driver growled something in a language that sounded like a pit bull arguing with Dr Doolittle. He swerved the hack rather violently across Third Avenue narrowly missing a little Korean on a bicycle.

'Allah be praised,' I said. I saw six thousand years of bad karma staring back at me through the rearview mirror.

When the pilgrimage finally ended at the near corner of 83rd Street I realized I didn't want to stay in the cab but I sure as hell wasn't eager to get out and see whatever Cooperman wanted to show me in Uptown Judy's apartment.

'Where're you from?' I asked as I gave him a twenty dollar bill.

'Tel Aviv, man,' he said.

Country *did* start with an 'I'.

'Shalom, brother,' I said as I got out of the cab. 'Keep the change.'

I walked up 83rd until I came to a familiar building. I wondered, do we ever really know the people we know? I pushed a buzzer, got buzzed in, and, taking the familiar elevator up to the third floor, began to lose my buzz. I walked down a familiar hallway. Do we ever know shit?

A slightly bored uniform was standing in front of Judy's door.

'Can I help you?' he asked. It was always a funny thing to say. A cop could say it in death's doorway. A salesperson could say it at Bergdorf-Goodman's. Not so long ago I could've said it to Tom Baker or Uptown Judy.

The uniform stuck his head into the apartment, exchanged a few muffled words with someone inside, then opened the door for me and melted out of the way.

The sweet and sour smell of death still hung in the heavy air as palpably as a christ on a cross. The whole apartment looked trashed – closets ransacked, drawers hanging out like tongues trying to tell you something. Even the door to the refrigerator was open.

Standing in the middle of the disarray was Detective Sergeant Mort Cooperman. The serpentine figure of Detective Sergeant Buddy Fox was studying the contents of the open refrigerator. Two techs were busy photographing the floor, dusting the furniture, and performing various other arcane procedures which only a mad scientist in a Walt Disney movie would understand.

Uptown Judy was nowhere to be seen.

Cooperman motioned me to follow him into the bedroom. I swallowed hard and walked in. The bedroom had also been tossed. No Judy.

'That look like her handwriting?' said Cooperman, nodding toward a bedside table. On the little table was a notepad. The top page had only one name and one phone number scrawled on it. Unfortunately, both were mine. I nodded to Cooperman. It did look like her handwriting.

I followed Cooperman back into the living room where the two techs were hunkered down near the middle of the floor. They were studying two faint but visible red lines across the wood that led to the door. Something about those lines caused the little hairs on the back of my neck to snap out of parade rest.

'Those're drag marks,' said Cooperman, matter-of-factly. 'Caused by a body being dragged along the floor. She must've been wearing a pair of red pumps or something. Can't find any in the apartment.'

'Cowboy boots,' I said. 'Red cowboy boots.'

Like a man in a dream I watched the two techs in their workmanlike fashion removing a small chip from the dark, dry stain on the floor, placing it in a glass tube of light blue liquid, holding it up to the light as it fizzed and bubbled and turned a darker color like a high school chemistry experiment, except it wasn't. The techs nodded at each other like two strangers on a commuter train. Then the guy holding the glass tube nodded at Cooperman and Cooperman nodded at him and I almost nodded out trying to decipher what was going on. Cooperman looked at me with a grim little smile ticcing lightly on his lips.

'It ain't Heinz 57,' he said.

7

Sergeant Cooperman had never been my idea of a father confessor figure. Sitting in Uptown Judy's apartment that night with the refrigerator door still standing wide open and with Cooperman across the little kitchen table instead of Uptown Judy was an extremely tedious experience at best.

The idea that Uptown Judy was dead, or at the very least, abducted and grievously wounded by God knows whom, was forcing me to sort out some thoughts of my own. Many of these I did not particularly wish to share with Sergeant Cooperman.

After all, the notion of having a relationship secretly and simultaneously with Uptown Judy and Downtown Judy that spanned several years was not especially wise or clever. It was more an admission of my own inability to love just one person. It was also a bit like sticking your kielbasa in a light socket while playing Russian roulette with the breaker switch.

For too long I'd condemned the two Judys to be more or less a station on the way. This did not make me proud to be an American.

'So you're fuckin' both these young ladies for two or three years on a fairly regular basis and they don't know about each other?'

'That's correct.'

'They both cared about you? Trusted you?'

'You'd have to ask them.'

'That may be a little difficult. How did you feel about them?'

'Who are you? Barbara Walters?'

Cooperman laughed a grating, malicious laugh. 'Just answer the questions. How did you feel about them?'

I wasn't in love with either of them, but I cared about both of them. Between the two of them they filled up an otherwise empty life. Sort of. And, of course, they cared about me in the normal perverse way women care about men who they think don't really give a damn.

'Nobody got hurt,' I said.

'Until now,' said Cooperman, lighting a cigarette with his zippo.

'What're the chances of finding Judy alive?'

'About the same as Hitler shavin' his mustache. Several hours ago a neighbor reported hearing a gunshot and a scream. You see what's left.'

Here Cooperman paused dramatically and gestured across the empty apartment. Fortunately, I reflected, I'd been right in the middle of someone at the time – well, actually not quite – but I'd been with someone earlier in the evening, so at least I wouldn't be one of the usual suspects – this time. But I still wanted to know more about what had happened. It was Cooperman, however, who was asking most of the questions.

'Where'd she work?'

'Madison Square Garden.'

'What'd she do?'

'I don't know.'

'Know anything about her family?'

'No.'

'Her background?'

'No.'

'Sounds like a deep relationship.'

'It had its moments.' Most of which, I reflected, were fairly horizontal.

'There is something you oughta know,' said Cooperman ominously. 'This broad's been in danger for some time. We always knew something like this could happen. I know you've got a tendency to snoop around in the area of crime now and then. You've had a little beginner's luck a few times out. You also almost got yourself polished a couple of times.'

'Why was Judy in danger?' I asked.

'Believe me, Tex, you don't want to know. This one you stay the fuck out of.'

Cooperman nodded and got up and it looked like our little chat was over. I had a lot of questions but, judging from his demeanor, I figured I'd save them for another time. I walked over to the door of the apartment and glanced back at the techs packing up their gear.

'You will let me know,' I said, 'when you find Judy?'

'You'll be the first on your block,' said Cooperman. 'Don't leave the city,' he shouted after me as I walked down the hall.

I'd had no great rapport with Cooperman in the past and it didn't look like things had gotten any better. He was a dedicated cop and he knew his job. I just didn't have any great confidence that he was going to find Uptown Judy very soon. And something in the back of my mind was telling me that very soon was not going to be fast enough.

I caught a hack and headed back down to the village. My thoughts were a troubled, jumbled embroidery of love, loneliness, distance, life and death. New York flashed by like the blurry, pastel view from a childhood carousel. Maybe, I thought, that's all it really was.

When I got back to the loft, Downtown Judy was still asleep. I didn't bother to wake her.

8

By the time I woke up Downtown Judy was gone and so were the dreamy shards of any youthful notion that life would go on forever. Like every other graffiti-strewn, ennui-driven subway train to nowhere, life would come to a screeching halt and all the passengers would have to get off. Anything left unsaid or undone would have to be forwarded to Fat Chance, Arkansas.

'Looks like a nice day,' I said to the cat. The cat could see that it looked like a perfectly hideous day, with a stultifying layer of gray over the city, out of which simultaneously emanated rain, sleet, snow, and every other inclement condition a postman prides himself in getting through.

The cat, of course, said nothing.

It was half past Gary Cooper time when Downtown Judy jumped through the blower on the right to ask me where the hell I'd run off to the night before. I asked her to give me a spiritual raincheck and I'd explain it to her over dinner at the Corner Bistro.

'Why can't you just tell me now?' she wanted to know.

'Because there is a large, old-fashioned wooden clothespin holding my lips together,' I said.

Judy went into a minor snit at that point and my mind was whirring with adequate lies to cover the situation. Our current level of understanding and communications was about the same as most married couples, I figured. At least, I had a reason for the subterfuge. Not only did I not want Downtown Judy to know about Uptown Judy's existence, now somewhat ironically, I had to also protect her from the knowledge of Uptown Judy's disappearance. The former knowledge would be merely unpleasant; the latter could be hazardous to her health.

'I'll tell you the whole story tonight,' I said, 'at the Corner Bistro.'

'You'd better,' she said.

Cooperman did not call. No one else did either which was fine with me. I suddenly had no desire to converse with the living. If Tom Baker or Uptown Judy had wanted to reach me on heaven's radio I'd have given them a big ten-four. But you can't very well loiter around your loft waiting to hear from dead people. Even Houdini's wife Beatrice had gotten tired of waiting for him to contact her as promised from the other side. 'Ten years is long enough to wait for any man,' she'd said.

At two o'clock I told the cat she was in charge and left the loft for my meeting with Legs at the Monkey's Paw. Walking up Vandam I couldn't believe the Bakerman was dead – that I wasn't going to meet Tom, just some friend of his I didn't know. It was going to take more getting used to than I was used to.

Moving briskly through cold, damp Village streets toward Sheridan Square, I began seeing two long red drag marks somewhere along some dim and distant horizon of my brain. I realized that wherever Tom Baker was, it was more than likely that Uptown Judy was now keeping him company. The afternoon was so chilly and brittle it seemed like New York might break like a heart. I hoped the two of them had dressed warm.

By the time I descended from Christopher Street into

the smokey bowels of the Monkey's Paw, the cold had
brought tears to my eyes. It was for that reason, possibly,
that I hadn't seen Mick Brennan, internationally acclaimed
photographer and trouble-maker, sitting at the bar. I was
soon made aware of his presence.

'Sit down here, mate,' he said. 'Let us pour a few pints
down your neck.' It looked like Mick had poured quite a
few down his own neck already.

I took a stool next to him and let him order the drinks.
The Monkey's Paw had seen better days, I thought, as I
glanced around at the seedy interior. So had I.

'Sorry to hear about your mate goin' South,' said
Brennan.

'Yeah,' I said, and I drank about seven gulps of
Guinness.

'You seem to be holding up. You can still fly a barstool.'

'I'm handling it well,' I said. 'Right now I'm happier
than about 90 per cent of all the dentists in America.'

Brennan laughed and ordered another round. 'If you do
top yourself,' he said, 'I could use that loft of yours for a
photographic studio. Always wanted a place in the
Village.'

'Well,' I said, 'It's a bit of a premature ejaculation just
yet.'

Brennan laughed again but his eyes were sad. He was
a good man to be with when death was in the air. He
didn't pander to it. During the Falklands War he'd covered
the Argentine mainland as a Brit photographer and he
didn't mind telling you about it several times an evening.
His repellent behavior could clear a room with the best of
them. But he was not without charm. And he had an
uncanny ability to know the news before it hit the papers.

I watched the door for Legs. I didn't know what the hell

he looked like, only that he had a funny name. Of course, he might be saying the same about me.

'I hear your old girlfriend Uptown Judy's disappeared,' said Brennan a bit too casually.

'How the hell do you already know that?' I said. 'It happened late last night and Cooperman was taking great pains to keep it away from the press and to keep me from snooping.'

'I'm afraid we never divulge our sources,' said Brennan. 'However, you might talk to a large Irishman with a large head.'

I walked over to the payphone by the doorway. I'd forgotten all about waiting for Legs. I called McGovern at the *Daily News*.

'Mike McGovern World Headquarters,' he said.

'MIT – MIT – MIT!' I said. That was our code for the Man in Trouble Hotline we'd established since McGovern had found a story about a guy in Chicago who'd been dead in his apartment for six months before anyone had found him. We weren't going to let that happen to us. Of course, in a manner of speaking, it already had.

'MIT is right,' said McGovern in a low serious whisper. 'You never told me Uptown Judy's last name.'

'It's Sepulveda,' I said. 'So what?'

'So her father was Don Sepulveda.'

'I don't care if her father was Sunset Boulevard.'

'It's not a name,' said McGovern. 'Her father was *Don* Sepulveda. He was rubbed out by the Columbo Family five years ago.'

9

I was one clean shirt away from hanging myself from a shower rod. It'd been a ball-dragger of a weekend. Still no word from Cooperman on Uptown Judy which I took to be a bad sign. Still no word from Legs which I took to be a tedious sign. I wasn't an Indian or a psychic; I didn't read signs. But I knew something very repellent was in the air and it probably wouldn't be long before it wafted into my loft.

That evening I called Cooperman but he was out. Probably walking his pet stomach or playing miniature golf or possibly staring stoically at Uptown Judy's puffy face looking up at him from an over-sized ice tray. With the background McGovern had given me, there was no way I could see a happy ending to Uptown Judy's story. Maybe Hollywood and the fairy tales had used so many happy endings there weren't any more in stock.

I left a message for Cooperman to call me but I wasn't going to hold my breath. There was damn little I could do about the situation. At the moment it seemed even risky talking about it more than absolutely necessary. If the same guys who'd polished Judy's father had also spliced her, they'd either had a hell of a long-time grudge or they were looking for something. They also had my name and phone number now from the pad in Judy's apartment. If they wanted any Sepulveda Family secrets from me, however, they were barking up the wrong disappearing rain forest. I'd known nothing about Judy's background. And the only secrets I'd ever kept were the ones I'd forgotten.

'Judy,' I said, as she stared expectantly at me through the candlelight and din of a back table at the Corner Bistro,

'I really wish I could tell you more about what happened last night.'

'How can you tell me *more*?' she asked reasonably. 'You haven't told me a thing yet.'

Downtown Judy's hazel eyes and red hair seemed to be burning with righteous anger. I knew 'I went to see a man about a dog' wasn't going to cut it. I looked her in the eyes and had to avert my gaze to the obscenely large Bistroburger on the plate before me.

'I didn't want bacon,' I said.

'What!'

'I told 'em to drag it through the garden but I didn't want bacon.'

'Listen! You tell me where the hell you went last night. Now!'

'I'll tell you. Just don't make a scene in here.' It would've been hard to make a scene in the Corner Bistro. Two hermaphrodites could hose each other right on the counter and not too many people would notice.

I couldn't tread water in the Rubicon much longer. I looked at Downtown Judy's face, now angry, but basically honest and trusting, and I tried to imagine Uptown Judy's features. I was amazed to find that I couldn't clearly remember what she'd looked like. Is that what happened when you died? You just blipped off the screen and people forgot you? It was also possible, I thought, that just as McGovern and I taken together pretty much represented an adequate human being, the two Judys taken together pretty much represented an adequate relationship for me. Not that I was all that demanding.

'Okay,' I said. I took a large bite of my Bistroburger and chewed it 97 times for good digestion. I nodded my head encouragingly at Judy so that she might do the same but

she continued to stare at me. No one likes social workers
to watch them while they eat.

'Okay,' I said. 'I got a call from Sergeant Cooperman, a
homicide dick. You were sleeping so peacefully I didn't
want to wake you.'

'Now we're getting somewhere,' Judy said, rubbing her
hands together like an insect. I recalled how interested
Judy'd been in some of the cases I'd been involved with
in the past. Possibly she saw herself as Nancy Drew and
me as Thomas Hardy or whatever the hell his name was.
Frank and Joe.

'Cooperman told me to come to a certain address – I
don't remember exactly – it was uptown – and he asked
me if I knew this person – '

'Who was the person?'

I took another bite of Bistroburger. It wasn't bad, even
with the bacon. I gave Judy a little gesture that indicated
I would swallow quickly and tell her what she wanted to
know or possibly I would need a Heimlich maneuver.
Unfortunately, I'd never been a very good liar. My only
chance, I figured, was to tell the story exactly as it happened but substitute another party for Uptown Judy. I
swallowed, took a nicely paced gulp of Prior's Dark, and
went on with it.

'There was a guy,' I said. 'Friend of Tom Baker's. Name
was Legs. He'd worked on a film with Tom which, by the
way, has turned up missing. Along with Tom, of course – '

'So you left the loft – '

'Went up to the address Cooperman had given me. To
the guy's apartment. The neighbors, apparently, had
reported that a shot had been fired. There was dried blood
on the floor. There were drag marks where someone'd
dragged the body out the door.'

'Wow,' said Judy enthusiastically. Heartened by her response, I continued.

'So Cooperman asked me how I knew the guy – '

'Wait a minute,' said Judy. 'Wait a minute.'

I waited.

'How did Cooperman know you knew Legs? Why would he call you?'

'Well,' I said, 'that part's kind of interesting, or maybe it's not, depending on how you look at it.'

'Just tell me, goddammit!' Judy was buying it but she wanted her money's worth.

'There was a pad of paper on a bedside table. The only thing on it was my name and phone number.'

'Jesus,' said Judy. In her mind she was probably getting her flashlight and parka out so the two of us could go about solving 'The Secret of the Old Mill'. Unpleasant. It was now my turn to toss down a little sidecar of Wild Turkey and watch Judy thoughtfully munching a Bistro-burger that was about the size of her head. The road to hell, I figured, was paved with social workers eating Bistroburgers.

After dinner, Judy and I went our separate ways, she vowing to help me solve the mysterious disappearance of Legs, and me promising to keep her posted on developments as I heard them from Cooperman. We probably would've spent the night together but it was still that time of the month and I was emotionally and spiritually wasted. Also, Judy had some kind of support group seminar she had to chair at some ungodly hour in the morning. As I walked up Vandam to the loft I reflected that one of the more attractive features dead people had going for them was that they didn't need support groups.

The phones were ringing as I opened the door to the

loft. I walked over to the desk, patted the cat, and gingerly picked up the blower on the left.

'Start talkin',' I said. It was Sergeant Cooperman and he did. He gave me an address and told me, not quite in these words, to get over there right away.

'Sergeant,' I said, 'you're starting to repeat yourself. You called me around this time last night and you wanted – '

'Get over here now,' he shouted. 'We got a notepad on the table with your name and number on it and this time we got a fuckin' stiff to go along with it.'

'Is it Uptown Judy?' I asked, not sure I really wanted to know. Still holding the blower, I hurriedly put my coat back on and grabbed three cigars for the road.

'Hell no it ain't Uptown Judy,' said Cooperman. 'It's a guy named Legs.'

10

Legs' apartment wasn't quite as nice as Uptown Judy's. What was inside it wasn't quite as nice either. I hadn't known what Legs had looked like before but, whatever that had been, he didn't look that good now. Where one of his eyes had been there now resided a crusty crater large enough to house a small grapefruit. Just glancing at the wound was enough to make you not wish to think of grapefruit. It rather put one off one's nice fried kippers. The eye that was still in Legs' head was brown and sensitive and looking right at me.

'Don't you normally close the eyes or something?' I asked Cooperman.

'If we can find 'em,' said Cooperman. 'Your name seems to be poppin' up a lot lately.'

'That's the price of fame,' I said.

Cooperman looked at me malevolently. He was not pleased. One of the techs from the night before seemed to recognize me and looked up briefly. When he saw Cooperman's demeanor he went back to work. Cooperman went back to glaring at me with dead cop eyes that were only slightly less unnerving than Legs' Cyclopean gaze.

'Take a good look, Tex,' said Cooperman, indicating the rather obvious stiff on the floor of the little apartment. 'What does this look like to you?'

I tiptoed a little closer to the body. I don't know why people always walk quietly around stiffs. Stiffs could give a damn. Maybe supposedly live people are afraid some of the supposed death will rub off. I didn't answer Cooperman.

'See the entry wound there behind the left ear?' Cooperman pointed it out to me like a guy explaining a dishwasher. 'See the exit wound where the right eye used to be?'

'Yeah.' Legs' good eye seemed like it was trying to say something. Whatever it was would keep, I guess.

'What's it look like to you?' asked Cooperman. 'I mean with your vast experience in the criminal field, I'm sure you can shed some light on this.'

From the other side of the room Fox laughed a nasty laugh. The sick little smile lit Cooperman's face briefly then was gone like a twitch. When two dicks want to get hard with you they quite often start out with what they think is funny. It's best to play along with them, I've found. Be a good sport. They can always take the ball and go home and, very possibly, it might be one of yours.

'Looks like a garden variety execution-style wing de-icing,' I said.

'Very good,' said Cooperman with sarcastic icing of his own you could've cut with a plastic birthday cake knife.

32

'Execution-style,' he nodded at Fox. Fox nodded back and beamed at me.

I took the compliment graciously and glanced around the place. It had been tossed and trashed much in the manner of Uptown Judy's.

'Whatever these guys are looking for,' I said, 'I wish they'd hurry up and find it.'

I also wished Cooperman and Fox would hurry up and let me get out of there. I hadn't brought my toilet kit and I didn't want to have to ask Cooperman if I could borrow his toothbrush. It was at least two hours before I was allowed to bug out for the dugout and drink myself into oblivion on a bar stool at the Monkey's Paw.

The story of my searching for the missing documentary on Elvis impersonators sounded phony even as I told it to Cooperman and Fox. God knows how it played with them. The fact that my name and phone number had been prominent at both murder scenes seemed to be about the only obvious lead they had and they were damned if they were going to let go of it. It seemed fairly logical to me. Uptown Judy hadn't seen me in a while and she was planning to call me. Legs was just returning my calls regarding getting together to discuss the Elvis film's disappearance. Cooperman and Fox didn't quite see it this way.

They felt that two in a row wasn't good. That I must, in some impalpable way, be inextricably bound to both incidents. They thought there must be something I wasn't telling them. If I knew what the hell it was I would've hired the Goodyear Blimp.

Later, at the Monkey's Paw, with Tommy pouring me a succession of shots of Jameson's, I wondered about a few things myself. They say drinking hinders thinking but that's only partially true. Practically all of the first rank Pulitzer Prize-winning novelists in our country have also been horrific piss artists. This has to count for something. It might mean that life itself is so hideously twisted and convoluted that only a drunk can effectively attach or convey any real meaning to it. There's more dead doctors than there are dead drunks and I hoped things remained that way. It wasn't much fun drinking with dead doctors. Unless they were Dr Seuss.

I couldn't for the life of me see any connection between the two incidents, other than my name and phone number and the fact that both times someone had been looking for something. A lot of people are looking for something. Most of the time, of course, they never find it. But at least it keeps them on their toes until they grow up and get to be a dead doctor. The Jameson's was really starting to kick in.

By the time I left the Monkey's Paw I was confused, depressed, thoroughly demoralized, and practically walking on my knuckles. I was a man without a zip code. It was a good way to start the week.

11

Legs' eyeball was still staring at me the next morning from my espresso cup. In a macabre sort of way I was starting to feel I knew the guy. It was not a particularly healthy sensation. Of course, interpersonal relations had never been my long suit.

Later in the morning Ratso called and managed to insinuate himself into what I liked to think of as my life. When he walked into the loft with the puppet head in one hand and half a pastrami sandwich in the other, he seemed to have a very determined Watson-like gait.

'So tell me,' he said, as he took a chair near the desk, 'about these skid marks on Uptown Judy's floor.'

34

'Drag marks, Ratso,' I said. 'Not skid marks. Skid marks are what you have on that old sofa in your apartment.'

'Mike Bloomfield and Phil Ochs never complained about it.' He started in on his sandwich.

Michael Bloomfield was a great rock guitarist and Phil Ochs had been a seminal folk singer of the sixties. Both had gone to the pearly gates, no doubt eased along, at least in part, by the skid marks on Ratso's couch.

'No,' I said, lighting a cigar, 'I'm sure they didn't. Mind if I smoke?'

'Go right ahead,' he said, as half his head disappeared in a cloud of blue-gray smog.

I asked Ratso how he knew about the drag marks and he told me he'd heard it from Brennan. Brennan had probably heard it from McGovern. It looked like the Village Irregulars were at it again. No point in trying to keep things quiet if the whole damn town already knew about it. And to be perfectly fair, Ratso, McGovern and Brennan had all contributed significantly to cases I'd worked on in the past. Rambam and Boris had saved my ass a couple times, too, though I hoped this time things wouldn't go that far.

'What else do you know?' I asked Ratso casually.

'I know Judy was shot and dragged from her apartment and is now most likely dead.' He masticated rather unpleasantly for a long moment. 'Sorry, man,' he said.

'Well, you know, it's been a long time since Judy and I were close – if we ever were. I knew her mostly during my blue period – '

'You mean when you were fucked up.'

'I prefer to say slightly amphibious.'

'I'm surprised you remember anything,' said Ratso, shaking his head in disgust.

'Oh, I remember, all right.' I took a somewhat pontifical

puff on the cigar and looked quizzically at Ratso. 'What was your name again?' I said.

I was not particularly upset that Ratso, McGovern and Brennan knew about Uptown Judy. About the only person who didn't know was Downtown Judy. When the body was found and the news finally hit the papers big-time I might have to do some rather intricate explaining. In the meantime, I had enough trouble figuring the damn thing out for myself.

What the hell. If Ratso knew about Uptown Judy he might as well know about Legs. Sherlock would've told Dr Watson. Nero Wolfe would've told Archie Goodwin. Besides, Ratso was an expert on Bob Dylan, Jesus and Hitler. In his apartment were over ten thousand books that in some arcane way dealt with the lives of these three timeless troublemakers. Ratso was precisely the kind of guy that might be able to shed some light on Elvis and his legion of impersonators.

So I told Ratso that both Tom Baker's film and Legs' eyeball were now missing. Both items were, apparently, news to him, though he had discussed the film with Baker some time ago.

'Baker was telling me something about it but I can't remember exactly what. Anyway, Elvis doesn't quite belong in a league with Jesus, Hitler and Bob Dylan.'

'And he certainly doesn't belong in a league with you. That'd be *20,000 Leagues Under The Sea*.'

I poured us each a cup of espresso and found an old half-smoked cigar in the waste basket. I fired it up with a mucus-colored Bic that had been in the family for about forty-eight hours.

'Resurrecting a dead cigar always gives me a little buzz,' I confided to Ratso.

'That's probably how Lazarus felt when he saw Jesus on the fifth day.'

I puffed a few times and looked admiringly at the cigar stub. 'Very possibly,' I said.

About two hours after Ratso had departed the phones rang. I went for the blower on the left.

'Start talkin',' I said.

'It's Ratso.'

'Long time between dreams.'

'Yeah, well I thought you'd want to know. I remembered what Baker told me about the film. He was saying that he was going through some kind of real weirdness with these impersonators. He seemed really shook up about it.'

'Pardon the expression.'

'He said the way things were going, before he finished the film he might be meeting Elvis.'

12

Early that evening I was trudging up Vandam Street returning from a shopping spree. I was carrying two bags full of cat food, cigars, and toilet paper – all the essentials. The sky looked like it might snow but didn't really give a damn. I was wearing a heavy coat, cowboy hat, and hunting vest with cigars stuffed in the little stitched loops instead of shot gun shells. That didn't mean I wasn't going hunting. Actually, it might have to be more like poaching. Especially if Cooperman was never going to declare the season open.

As I climbed onto the freight elevator in what passed for the lobby of the building, I thought again of the comment Tom Baker had made to Ratso. I watched the one exposed light bulb sway slightly back and forth and remembered something Captain Midnite had once told me about Elvis. Midnite had known Elvis since Christ was a cowboy. He contended that Elvis had been turned into a chemical puppet very early on through drugs given him by bluegrass and gospel groups who were, for all practical purposes, out where the buses don't run. By the time Elvis hit it big, he had enough stock to open his own Walgreens.

Stepping out of the elevator onto the fourth floor I heard a strange high-pitched yapping noise coming from the stairwell. Two small dogs, one white and one brown, headed straight toward me and began running madly around in tiny concentric circles of hell at my feet.

'So they're not squirrels,' I said to the footsteps coming up the stairs.

The footsteps were auditorially attached to the longest legs I'd ever seen in my relatively short life. It was the beautiful blonde from the county fair.

'They're not squirrels,' she said, 'but evidently you are.'

There's very little that any faintly heterosexual male can say to a woman that breath-taking. And I didn't. Fortunately, she carried on the conversation.

'This is Pyramus,' she said, pointing to the brown one who was tugging at my jeans. 'And this is Thisbe.' Thisbe was trying to flatten herself like a tortilla and slide under my doorsill. The cat, who I could hear on the other side, was not amused.

'What kind of dogs are they?' I said when I got my voice back. This girl was really killer bee.

'I'm so glad you asked,' she said with a sort of sexy sarcasm as she smiled down at me. She was wearing heels and she looked to be about nine foot three.

'I should've worn my brontosaurus foreskin cowboy boots,' I said.

She looked at me again. 'It wouldn't have helped,' she said. She smiled and I knew she was right.

'Well, they're very cute little boogers, whatever kind of dogs they are.' I'd had some experience with tall people who owned little pets – or rather animal companions – and the little ones were absolutely the way to the big one's hearts. Still, there was something almost poignant about this statuesque beauty's obvious attachment to her two little animal companions. I wouldn't've minded trading places with either one of them as long as I could still smoke cigars.

'You're a cute little booger, too,' I said.

'C'mon girls,' she said as she started up the stairs for the fifth floor. Her two animal companions followed faithfully. This was one of those rare situations where the view from the rear was at least as good as the view from the front.

About halfway up the flight she turned and fixed me with an almost biblical blue-eyed gaze. Nobody turned into a pillar or anything but it sure made me want to lick her salt block.

'Pyramus is a yorkie,' she said, 'Thisbe is a maltese, and *you* are a fuckball.'

I summoned up all the talent I had in initiating relationships with truly beautiful women which, rather unfortunately, was little.

'That's Mr Fuckball to you,' I said.

She came very close to laughing, I thought, but apparently, decided against it and walked on up to the fifth floor. I heard a door being unlocked, opened, closed, and locked again, kind of like my heart.

Emily once wrote: 'Hope is the thing with feathers that perches in the soul.' Well, hope was flappin' like a November turkey at the moment.

And I damn well didn't want it to come to roost in Winnie Katz's loft.

13

Later that night as I was relaxing in my loft, having a little liquor drink to cut the phlegm, I found myself listening now and then for little yapping noises in the hallway. The yapping noises which had once seemed like somebody was piercing me with white hot needles, I now thought of as music from the baby Jesus's own little Jew's harp. Of course, I don't know what I'd have done had they come to pass my doorway. I thought of several possible opening lines. 'Now which one's the yorkie again?' 'Would you like to come in and meet my puppet head?' 'Did you know you got a bull dyke living across the hall?' At least I hoped she was across the hall.

I poured another shot to celebrate my good luck concerning the girl's geographic desirability. Quite cosmic, I thought, that she lived in the same building. I killed the shot and poured another and things seemed even more cosmic. I got up and put an old recording of *South Pacific* on the victrola. It was the original stage version featuring Mary Martin and Ezio Pinhead. Both of them, of course, had gone to Jesus, but their voices, perfectly mated spiritually, sang to me that night in such a celestial fashion as to make me almost wonder if I'd been along on the trip.

There is a story about Mary Martin that I often tell after four or five drinks. Usually after Mick Brennan's through telling his Falkland War stories. To the common man both of our ramblings would probably seem to be drunken, irrelevant, and frankly, rather tedious. But, as Thomas Jefferson used to say: 'Beware the common man.'

Mary Martin was arriving at LAX some years ago and her son, Larry Hagman, the J.R. of *Dallas* fame, was down to pick her up. Because of the bubble popularity of *Dallas*, swarms of fans were frantically beating their wings around J.R. and almost nobody noticed his frail mother descending from the corridor. As J.R. went forward to meet Mary, some of the crush of his rather boorish fans almost knocked her off her feet. To J.R.'s credit he caught Mary by the arm before she fell, just as Charles Manson reportedly once caught Squeaky Fromme by the arm before she fell. Manson's line at the time had been: 'I'll never let you fall.' J.R.'s line to Mary Martin was: 'Don't worry, mom. It's just showbusiness.'

That night, Mary Martin was to be honored at a gala dinner at the Century Plaza Hotel. Sir Laurence Olivier, Elizabeth Taylor, Cary Grant, Kirk Douglas, and anybody who was anybody on stage and screen were there resplendent in gowns and tuxedos. When Mary Martin was introduced, the crowd of over a thousand stood up as one and gave her an ovation that is said to have lasted for twenty minutes. During this ovation, Mary leaned over to J.R., who was also on the dais, and said: 'No, son, *this* is showbusiness.'

I killed a shot and poured another. If the squirrels were barking in the hallway I never would've known. Ezio Pinhead was transporting me and the cat with 'Some Enchanted Evening.' Of course, Hollywood did not deem Ezio Pinhead or Mary Martin worthy to star in the movie version. That's one reason the original stage version, if you can get it, is so much better than the movie soundtrack. Also, in the movie soundtrack, someone decided, in the song 'Bloody Mary', to take the phrase 'Her skin is tender as DiMaggio's glove' and transform it to 'Her skin is tender as a baseball glove'.

This change may seem minor but it is representative of Hollywood's take on a lot of things. The attitude is un-Italian, and un-American not to mention unmetrical. Paul Simon says: 'Where have you gone, Joe DiMaggio?' I wasn't sure where the hell he'd gone either. I just wanted to tell him: Don't forget to take your glove.

Around one in the morning I got a call from Downtown Judy. She sounded highly agitato. She'd read a story in the *Daily News*, McGovern no doubt, that Legs had been murdered the night before, and she'd been clever enough to realize that the killing had occurred *after* I'd told her about it at the Corner Bistro. She was coming over now and she wanted answers. I could've used a few myself.

I walked to the espresso machine, stoked it up, and kicked it into high gear. I fed the cat a midnight snack of tuna. The place had gotten a little chilly so I threw on an old purple bathrobe, lit another cigar, and paced a while. I didn't want to have to tell Downtown Judy about Uptown Judy but I didn't really see any easy way to avoid it. If Judy was going to be working with me and the other Village Irregulars she would find out sooner or later but I had a strong suspicion that later would be a lot more unpleasant.

I poured a cup of steaming espresso, noting with some relief that Legs' eyeball didn't appear to be an ingredient in the new batch, and I sat down at the desk with the cat waiting for the inevitable. The seeds we sow. Of course, nothing in life ever looks as good as it does on the seed packet.

'Time to face the music,' I said to the cat. The cat said nothing. It looked upward in the direction of a loud thudding that had begun to emanate from the ceiling of the loft. Winnie Katz's lesbian dance class was apparently conducting, possibly literally, some kind of nocturnal drill.

The cat appeared to be rather irritated with the noise. It flicked its tail violently from side to side. If I'd had a tail I'd have been doing that too, trying to decide whether to investigate the Uptown Judy case, search for the Elvis impersonator film, or kill Winnie Katz.

'Don't let it bother you,' I said to the cat finally. 'It's just showbusiness.'

14

By the time Downtown Judy walked into the loft, the only one smiling was the puppet head. Though anger indeed did serve to make Judy very attractive and sensual, it nonetheless wasn't something social workers like to hear. I kept the observation to myself. It was about all I'd be able to keep to myself, I figured. From the look on Judy's face it was past due for me to spit it.

Judy settled herself into the main chair behind the desk and gestured for me to sit in the guest's chair.

'No thanks,' I said, 'I'll pace. Care for an espresso?'

'No thanks,' she said sweetly. 'I'll just rip your heart out with my bare hands if you ever lie to me again like the other night.' Strong words for a social worker, but of course, I had better manners than to mention it. Also, I needed my heart for another decade or two, I thought. Otherwise, what would people have to break?

'There was a very good reason why I told you what I told you,' I said. Now, I thought, if I could just think what the reason was. I took a long time lighting a cigar. Then I walked determinedly over to the espresso machine and began drawing two cups.

'I don't want any espresso –'

'Hold the weddin' now, girl. We've got to have espresso

43

like all good little Turks before we discuss any really important matters of business.'

I made a great pretense of futzing around with the espresso machine and the two cups. Actually, I didn't know if the Turks drank espresso, Turkish coffee or Mr Pibb before discussing important matters of business. If they did, it was about the only thing I admired about them.

When Hitler's aides suggested to him that the world would never let him get away with murdering so many millions of Jews, he'd asked a simple question: 'Who remembers the Armenians?' he'd said.

I did. But the Turks had massacred over a million and a half Armenian men, women and children, and, like that pesky dental appointment, most of the world had forgotten it.

I handed her the cup of espresso which she received gracelessly. It made me wish for a moment that the Turks would massacre Downtown Judy.

'Look,' she said, 'I know you don't love me like you loved your girlfriend who died in Vancouver – What was her name?'

She'd kissed a windshield at about ninety miles an hour in her Ferrari and now it almost seemed like it'd happened in another lifetime. But those cracks in that windshield that I only saw in my nightmares had reverberated outward in ever-increasing timeless rainy night spider webs until one lazy afternoon they shattered my soul. These days it didn't seem to matter too much what I actually felt or who I really loved.

'Kacey,' I said.

I took a sip of hot bitter espresso. It tasted like tears. There was a distant yapping in the hallway.

'What was that?' asked Judy.

'New neighbor. Has a little dog.' Kacey'd told me about the dog they'd had when she was a child. It's name had been Pepper. Kacey and Pepper'd been together for a long time now.

'I'm your friend,' Judy said. 'Be straight with me. Tell me whatever's going on. Maybe I can help you.'

Maybe New Jersey would melt tomorrow. But her eyes seemed innocent of guile. What the hell.

'Okay,' I said.

I told her about Uptown Judy. About her existence, my relationship with her, her disappearance. Downtown Judy took it well.

'You're a pathetic, slow-leak, sniveling asshole,' she said, setting her espresso down with cold fury on the desk and staring at me as if I were a cockroach.

'Tell me what you really think,' I said. 'Don't hold it back.'

Judy leaned back in the chair and sighed a deep, troubled social worker's sigh. 'How was she?' she asked.

'How was who?'

'Goddammit, how was she?' she screamed, pounding the desk for emphasis. The cat enjoyed this prepubescent display almost as little as I did and jumped off the desk and onto the counter.

'Now you've done it,' I said. 'You've upset the cat.'

'The cat's going to be more upset when she sees your dick flying out the window.'

I puffed on the cigar and tried not to think Freudianly perverse auto-erotic thoughts. I needed to give Judy time to allow her temper to cool down at least to three-digit Celsius. Unconsciously, I walked over to the window, looked out at the street, and tried to collect my thoughts. What *was* she like?

I stood at the window for a long time until, almost in a

post-hypnotic trance, I began imagining I'd seen a pale, meteoric after-image of a dick sailing slowly down onto Vandam Street. At that point I turned and walked back to the desk. I told Judy the truth, if there was such an animal. No doubt on the extremely endangered list.

'She was nothing special,' I said, in what I hoped were soothingly sincere tones. 'I didn't love her. It was purely a physical thing. If I hadn't been fucked up as Grogan's goat I probably never would've touched her with a barge pole. Is that good enough?'

A strange expression briefly crossed her features. It could've been something almost akin to disappointment, or possibly simply anger in a quick fade to relief. Whatever it was, it was soon gone and she was in my arms and I was thinking of her in that very sexual, earthy, naturally nasty way that only certain redheads have the ability to engender in their prey. Like the insect on my bolo tie, I wondered if she'd eat the male after mating.

I went to sleep quite a while later with her taste on my lips and her scent in my nostrils and our bodies melded together. But when I dreamed, I dreamed of Kacey. Then I slept like a spent shell on the beach. If you'd held me to your ear you'd have heard the sound of the Pacific Ocean embracing the night-time California shoreline.

Sometime before dawn a noise awakened me. It sounded like it might've been the cat but instinctively, I didn't think so. Judy was still sleeping soundly beside me. I put on my sarong from Peace Corps days and wandered fuzzily into the living room. The cat was sleeping in her rocker. For the same reason a child looks under his bed, I went to the door of the loft, unlocked it, and opened it slowly.

Standing in the hallway was a pair of red cowboy boots.

15

Business was light at the cop shop that morning. I only had to wait about forty minutes on the wrong side of the pebbled glass to get an audience with Cooperman. I waited in the little foyer with my tall green plastic garbage bag that contained Uptown Judy's tall red cowboy boots. I felt like a rookie bag lady. I didn't know if fingerprints were possible on leather or drag marks could be matched up with the boot heels. I just had the feeling that the point of the whole exercise was to let me know in some mildly Sicilian way that everything was o-v-e-r as far as Uptown Judy was concerned. Someone seemed to be trying to tell me that I was wasting my time hoping to find her alive. At least I didn't have to wait around for the other shoe to drop.

When I did finally get in to see Cooperman he was not excited to see me and even less excited to see the cowboy boots. Fox wandered over from a nearby office and saw the red boots on Cooperman's desk.

'We'll have 'em ready for you on Friday,' he said.

'Look,' I said, 'they're definitely Judy's boots.'

'That's what you say now,' said Fox, 'but could you pick 'em out in a line-up?' Cooperman either laughed or coughed. Whichever it was was equally mirthless. The whole situation was fresh out of mirth.

'Can't you run a lab test on 'em? Match 'em with the drag marks?'

'Fuckin' A – Tweety,' said Cooperman. 'We'll jump right on it. We won't let the little fact that the boss has taken us off the case and given us another one as top priority

47

influence us at all. There ain't even a fuckin' stiff in this case.'

'Gotta have a stiff,' said Fox, smiling.

'Legs didn't look too shabby in the stiff department,' I said. I started to light a cigar.

'Don't smoke that in here,' said Fox. 'We got new regulations. No Jewish cowboys can smoke cigars in homicide. The passive smoke could cloud our thought processes in solvin' all these murders.'

'Anything else you'd like?' said Cooperman. 'Maybe some nice sliced apples and cheese?'

'I'd like to know if Legs had possession of Tom Baker's film on Elvis impersonators. I don't know why but I think these two murders are related. I don't know whether Judy knew Legs but she was friends with Tom Baker, the guy who made the film.'

Cooperman leaned back in his chair. He shook a Gauloises out of a crumpled pack, lit it with his Zippo, and coolly blew the smoke at me. 'I've got a theory on this,' he said, in a tone of deep confidentiality. 'We may be dealing with an Elvis impersonator who killed a Judy impersonator and you're an amateur detective impersonator who may end up worm bait.'

Fox clapped his hands. His eyes lit up with a reptilian glee. 'Then we'll have a stiff!' he said.

Walking home from the Sixth Precinct in a cold, light rain, I pondered the next step in the labyrinth. Bringing the boots to the cops had gone over like a turd in a bottle of Evian water. I should've given them to Ratso. He had a penchant for dead men's shoes. Maybe he'd like dead men's boots. Dead *person's* boots. The politics of it all didn't matter quite as much, of course, when you were dead. When you were a stiff it didn't matter if they called you Ms or His Holiness the Pope, or 'Hey, you!' It wasn't exactly a death wish but I found myself mildly looking forward to going to Jesus, albeit, in a rather offbeat, cerebral way.

My cowboy hat liked the rain and so did I. It was almost beginning to clear my mind and give my soul a Waylon Jennings Bus Shower which is where you splash water from a sink under your armpits and other appropriately funky areas and hope for the best.

The linkage in the two murders was now quite obvious to me. Both victims had known Tom Baker. Both had been shot, though no bullet was recovered at Judy's place to match with the one Legs had caught. Still, it was the same modus operandi – shot with a gun, apartment trashed because someone was looking for something. Also, both victims had been meaning to or attempting to contact yours truly.

Patterns were emerging in my mind that the NYPD was not taking the time to see. How I wished that instead of Cooperman and Fox, I could have dealt with Inspector Maigret of the Paris police. With Inspector Maigret beside me, walking in the rain, hands thrust into the pockets of his ancient frog overcoat that was now coming into fashion in the States, smoking his old pipe, quite possibly upsidedown, in the rain – with Maigret beside me, the two of us could seine the frantic human kaleidoscope of the city – any city, no matter how big or cold or busy; we could find the time to make things rhyme – little things that one day would hang the murderer from a gibbet.

Now I felt Maigret walking with me. I could not see his face – no one ever has – but I could feel his mind. Gravely, with deep humanity, it was processing permutations and possibilities that computers could only dream of. Maigret was an expert in human nature. Human nature was the skeleton key to open the gates of the white castle, to reveal the secrets in the blackest mind.

Maigret left me at the freight elevator. He wandered out onto Vandam Street and vanished into smoke and rain. I knew what I had to do. It was time to forget about technicians, ballistics labs, beakers of blood. It was time to put on my lobster bib and call a formal meeting of the Village Irregulars.

16

At two o'clock the following afternoon I addressed the multitudes who stood assembled in my loft. I intoned the words of Wavy Gravy: 'Mistakes are good. We like mistakes. They mean we're human.'

'Cut the shit, mate,' said Mick Brennan. 'Tell us what we're here for.'

'If you'll be quiet and give him a chance,' said Downtown Judy rather stridently, 'he'll try to tell you.'

From the forest of Guinness bottles near the neighborhood of where McGovern and Brennan were sitting, the word 'cunt' was heard to be muttered rather distinctly. Judy visibly tensed; nonetheless it did seem to have the rather gratifying effect of having her pull her lips together.

'Pardon the Shakespeare,' I said, pouring myself a medicinal shot of Jameson's.

Rambam looked on in bored amusement from near the doorway. As a private investigator, he was the only one in the room with even the nuance of any professional training in the field, and it was not clear how he would suss out the little scenario. I wanted to draw him in because, unorthodox and both-sides-of-the-law as he was, if things got ugly we'd certainly need him.

Pete Myers had catered the affair from his gourmet British food shop, if there is such a thing, Myers of Keswick on Hudson Street. He'd laid out a fine spread of pork pies, pasties, mashers, bashers, other things with weird names, and sausages that tasted killer bee but you didn't want to ask too many questions about them. Ratso, of course, had established squatter's rights in a chair adjacent to the Myers of Keswick table. Myers himself was deftly slicing a beautiful chunk of red roast beef almost as large as McGovern's head.

'Let's take it from the top,' said Ratso. 'Tell it from the beginning. We all need to be on the same wavelength.'

'Good luck,' I heard Rambam mutter from the doorway, and I began my recounting of the facts as I knew them. Not surprisingly, it didn't take very long.

'In summing up,' I said, 'we want to find the killer of Judy and Legs and find the Bakerman's missing film about Elvis impersonators. I'm pretty well convinced that when we find one we'll find the other.'

'Got another pork pie over there, mate?' Brennan called out.

'Ratso ate all of them,' said Myers.

'Rotten luck,' Brennan said.

'Look,' said McGovern, 'I've got a deadline here. Let's go ahead and get a division of labor going that's a little more effectual than the way we divided up the pork pies.'

Ratso, looking sated and rather sullen, nonetheless retorted gamely. 'These fuckin' pork pies have been sitting here for over two and a half hours. Irish people like to drink, Jewish people like to eat. I don't know what British people like to do.' At this last, Ratso stared pointedly in Brennan's direction.

'We like to complain about Irish people and Jewish

people,' said Brennan. 'Like what's a Jew doing eating pork?'

'Anti-semitism rears its ugly head,' said Ratso with an almost Gandhi-like dignity.

'Boys!' said Judy sharply. 'You all have various talents and skills. We'll need your cooperation to get to the bottom of this. McGovern's a fine, experienced reporter, Mick is an internationally recognized photographer – '

'Yeah,' said Ratso. 'He can keep the scrapbook.'

'You can keep your mouth shut, mate,' said Brennan. For every pork pie Ratso had scarfed, Brennan had poured a bottle of Guinness down his neck. If there'd been an entry in the Guinness Book of Records for drinking Guinness, Brennan was in the hunt.

'Rambam is a registered private investigator,' Judy continued. 'I'm sure he'll be helpful.' Rambam lifted a glass of whatever he was drinking in a mock toast to the assembled group.

'Your immediate death,' he said. Then he took a drink, swallowed, and belched rather loudly. He didn't say anything else but his eyes roved menacingly around the circle of faces. It did not appear from his demeanor that he would be as helpful as Judy had hoped.

'And Ratso,' said Judy. There was an uncomfortable pause as she struggled to pinpoint what it was that Ratso would do to help the group. Ratso looked crestfallen and I felt it was time to take the baton from Judy if possible.

'Ratso's already been very helpful to me,' I said. 'He knew Tom Baker well, as all of you did, and he's provided me with some interesting insights. If any of you remember anything else Baker did or something he said to you that might shed some light on these mysterious matters, please don't fail to call it to my attention in the arduous days ahead.'

'What's she gonna do?' Brennan inquired loudly of the Guinness bottle sitting in front of his nose.

'Judy's a trained social worker who'll be working to keep the rest of us from de-balling each other. She'll be working closely with me.'

'Very closely,' said McGovern. He laughed his loud, almost obscene Irish laugh, which always seemed a little too loud for indoor use.

'Okay,' I said. The group was starting to get a little restless, not to say stultifyingly bored. 'McGovern, you research the relationship between Judy and her dad, Don Sepulveda. Anything you find on him will be helpful. Mick, you stay tuned. We're going to need your services before this is over.'

'I won't leave the city,' slurred Brennan.

'Ratso,' I continued. 'You keep digging on the little Elvis research project we discussed earlier. Give Hitler, Jesus, and Bob Dylan a rest. Concentrate on Elvis.'

'I'll try to find some information on Elvis's last British tour,' said Ratso.

'Elvis never played the UK, mate,' said Brennan.

'I know that,' said Ratso. 'He was probably afraid he'd run into your ass.'

'And Judy,' I said, 'I'd like to thank you for taking copious notes on this meeting. If you'll stick around afterwards I have something in mind for you.' McGovern laughed again, louder, if possible, than before. Judy looked down at the big chief tablet I'd given her which had a few notations on it that looked like they'd been written by a spider. She smiled bravely.

'And finally,' I said, 'Rambam. Do you have any last words for us?' Everyone looked at Rambam who walked slowly around the counter and approached the group. He was dressed in suit and tie, possibly over-dressed for the occasion, especially when compared to Ratso who seemed to be wearing Sonny Bono rejects. Rambam assumed the demeanor of one who was about to address a group of killer Kiwanians.

'I'm going to take our esteemed leader on a building sweep tomorrow – '

'He doesn't do windows,' said Ratso.

Rambam continued smoothly. ' – Of the two murder sites. For the rest of you. There is a killer out there. We don't know who it is. But very soon he'll start to know who we are. The cops won't help us on this and they sure aren't going to save our ass. So be forewarned.'

Rambam fixed the little group with a cold eye. 'You may be the Village Irregulars, but this is some dangerous shit.' He paused and straightened his tie for dramatic effect. Everyone waited.

'Don't think you can just reach for the Metamucil,' he said.

17

If Cinderella thought sweeping a building was tedious she should've tried working with Rambam. He worried the occupants of Uptown Judy's apartment house like the Hound of the Baskervilles gnawing on Yorick's skull and then some. Many of them no doubt were wishing they'd seen or heard something just to get Rambam's foot out of their doorway.

'They didn't waste any time renting out Judy's apartment,' I said to Rambam as we reached the third floor.

'Landlords love to cut through those scene-of-the-crime banners like politicians enjoy snipping ceremonial ribbons.

Head 'em up. Move 'em out. In the language of your people.'

'Jesus Christ, Rambam, we're not even sure Uptown Judy's dead.'

Rambam gave me a look that would've withered a flower pressed in a book containing the poetry of John Keats. '*Some* of us aren't sure,' he said.

He handed me a walkie-talkie and knocked on Judy's door. Judy didn't answer. Nobody else did either.

'New tenant's probably out buying a throw rug to cover the drag marks,' said Rambam with a little smile. We walked over to the apartment to the left of Judy's and Rambam knocked again.

'Who is it?' came a voice that sounded like an inebriated macaw.

'Investigators,' said Rambam.

'What do you want?' cried the voice.

'To investigate,' said Rambam.

I held my walkie-talkie and waited. A lock clicked on the other side of the door. Then another lock.

Rambam leaned toward me and said softly: 'White, early sixties, two hundred pounder, wearing floral houserobe that hasn't been washed in twenty years.'

A chain was unlatched from inside the door and then it opened. Even through a thin veil of cigar smoke I could smell the fetid creature. She bore an uncanny resemblance to Rambam's description except that there were no flowers on the bathrobe. Phlegm-colored goldfish appeared to be swimming in its massive and murky folds, fighting like hell not to go belly-up.

'Wait one minnow,' I said. 'Something's fishy.'

'It's him what done it,' she shouted, pointing across the hallway to the apartment directly opposite hers.

'Him what done what?' Rambam inquired. The

woman's whole apartment smelled like dying goldfish. I thought very briefly of Dale Haufrect, the childhood neighbor who'd once killed my goldfish and taught me my first lesson in mortality. Dead creatures stay dead. I thought of Judy's red cowboy boots standing at the front door of my loft. Could they not conceivably indicate that Judy was alive just as well as dead? On the other hand, or foot in this case, if she were alive, wouldn't it be more likely that she would be in them? Instead of rotting like a dead goldfish somewhere in the East River?

'It's him and his goddamn microwave what's puttin' these water blisters on my nose,' said the woman.

Even Rambam didn't have an immediate answer for that one. He did, however, lean slightly closer to her nose to observe that it did, indeed, contain a rather unsavory network of water blisters.

'Have you thought about taking some tinfoil and making a little shield and wearing it on your nose?' Rambam said. Now we were getting somewhere, I thought.

'That might be a good idea,' the woman told Rambam. I told him it might be a good idea if we tried another apartment.

Before we departed, Rambam asked the woman at last about the night in question. She maintained adamantly that she had seen nothing unusual that night and had heard nothing from the apartment next door.

'Curious,' said Rambam, as we walked past Judy's former home and approached the apartment to its immediate right.

'Not to say unpleasant,' I added. I'd long known New Yorkers had a reputation for being somewhat eccentric, but the water-blister woman was definitely out where the buses don't run.

Rambam knocked on the door of the other bookend to Judy's place. As he waited for an answer he said: 'You did say Cooperman told you there'd been a call to 911 about a shot having been fired?'

'Ten-four,' I said into the non-functional walkie-talkie, just as the door opened and a slight white male in a pastel-colored floral kimono squinted out at the two of us.

'Hi,' he said, with a smile that was far too friendly for a New York heterosexual.

'There's my floral houserobe,' said Rambam, with a slight hint of triumph in his voice.

'You can have it if you want it,' said its owner invitingly. 'Why don't you guys come inside for some banana bread and brie? But leave that smelly cigar in the hall.' He wrinkled his nose in an exaggerated fashion that might've been sexy if he'd been a pretty young girl from Texas. Hell, maybe he was a pretty young girl from Texas.

'Can't leave the cigar in the hall,' I said. 'I might have an anxiety attack.'

He scrunched-up his nose again. 'Well, why don't *you* come in and let your friend go smoke his big ol' smelly cigar somewhere else?'

'We're investigators,' said Rambam. 'We've got to do the whole building.'

The guy's face lit up. 'If you're gonna do the whole building, why not start right here!'

'That's not what I meant,' said Rambam. 'We want to know if you noticed anything – loud noises, a gunshot, sounds of a struggle, any strange men – having to do with the apartment next door earlier in the week.' Rambam gestured with his head toward Judy's flat in an effort to help the guy remember.

' – Any strange men?' the guy asked himself out loud. The guy obviously was stymied. He was shaking his head rather wistfully either indicating he'd seen and heard nothing or that he wished he had so Rambam would come inside his apartment.

He kept shaking his head, pursing his lips, and occasionally, glancing over at me and wrinkling his nose. He was starting to get up my sleeve.

'Just the facts, ma'am,' I said.

Rambam looked at me with a gaze of cool amusement, then ran it all down with the guy again, coming up empty just as before.

'I hope you'll come back when you're through investigating. Maybe I'll remember something,' he teased.

'Nice housecoat,' said Rambam, as we moved on to the next apartment and knocked on the door.

Hours later, in a trendy little bar along Third Avenue, Rambam and I were dusting off some of the cinders from the building sweep. I was having a Vodka McGovern and Rambam was sipping the most arcane and expensive cognac in the house. Rambam was in a slightly more positive and optimistic frame of mind than I was. So were Kafka and Edgar Allan Poe.

'Jesus Christ,' I said. 'Now I can truly empathize with Jehovah's Witnesses.'

'Don't get too fucked-up. We still got to sweep Legs' building.'

'But what the hell are we accomplishing? Nobody claims to have seen or heard a thing. Maybe everybody in the building's autistic.'

'This is what most detective work is all about. But it's very interesting to me that none of the people we interviewed seems to remember anything pertinent about the night in question.'

'None of the people we interviewed would've remembered the Hindenburg if it fell on their head.'

'That's true,' said Rambam, offering me a sip of his drink. It was the kind of cognac that was so expensive it smelled like somebody's feet. It didn't taste too bad but after two Vodka McGoverns bile doesn't taste too bad.

'The people in that building remind me of that dog in the Sherlock Holmes story,' said Rambam.

'Oh yeah, I know the one. You mean that rottweiler that Sherlock's brother Mycroft tried to command to have sexual relations with Dr Watson?'

Rambam laughed. 'No,' he said. 'I was thinking of the time Sherlock solved the mystery because of the clue of the dog that didn't bark.'

'You know what I think?'

'Of course I do but tell me anyway.'

'Give me another sip of that Louis the whatever-the-fuck-it-is and I'll tell you.'

'It's Louis the Thirteenth and it's only about sixty dollars a glass but help yourself.'

I took a healthy swallow this time. It did taste better than bile. I took another swallow and Rambam grabbed his appropriately stemmed glass back from my hand.

'So what the fuck do you think?' he said.

'I think that same dog might've called 911.'

18

The occupants of Legs' building in the Village were equally tedious but slightly more forthcoming than the ones in Judy's building. Not that Legs or Judy gave a damn. Of course, in Legs' case many had seen the body being carried out by the coroner's men and most had read accounts of the murder in the papers. In Judy's case, they were still

wearing little tinfoil shields on their noses. In both loci it
hadn't been a banner day for building sweeps.

'Maybe we should've been chimney sweeps,' I said to
Rambam, as we hauled ass out of the building with the
super threatening to call the cops.

'Wait a minute,' said Rambam in the little foyer. 'What's
this?'

'Whatever it is I'm sure it'll still be here when we come
back in the year 2007.'

Rambam was looking at the row of rusty mailboxes built
into the wall like homes for Lilliputian cliff-dwellers. He
took something out of his pocket that looked like a putty
knife.

'Why don't you just loiter in the lobby for a while?' said
Rambam.

'This *is* the lobby,' I said. I looked around nervously for
the super but he seemed to have blipped off the screen.
Probably had to get back to *Barnaby Jones.*

'Why don't you loiter in that lesbian bar across the street.
This shouldn't take long. Looks like the dear departed
received some recent correspondence that the NYPD hasn't
monitored too carefully.'

'Hard to believe.' I watched Rambam begin to jimmy
with the mailbox. 'I can't loiter in that lesbian bar across
the street. I tried one night and they wouldn't let me in.'

'Seems like you've got a good discrimination suit you
could bring against them. "Kinky Friedman vs The Cubby
Hole". You should talk to Wolf Nachman. He's the greatest
lawyer in the world.'

'I'd like to talk to you about hurrying up with that
fucking putty knife.'

At that moment a middle-aged guy, kind of non-descript
for New York, came in the front door and started futzing
with his own mailbox about four feet away from Rambam.

Rambam turned his body slightly in an effort to hide the putty knife, but the guy hardly noticed. He looked like an accountant or serial killer-type. Definitely one of the service industries.

'One of these days they'll fix these mailboxes,' Rambam said to the guy. I laughed in a good-natured way and wished the lesbians would've let me loiter in the bar across the street.

The guy paid no attention to me or Rambam. Just got his mail and went upstairs.

'That's one advantage New York's got over everywhere else,' said Rambam. 'Nobody cares enough to be nosy.'

'Yeah,' I said. 'It's kind of refreshing, isn't it?'

Rambam opened the box, removed a small stack of letters and bills, and placed them in my hand.

'Just remember,' he said, 'you didn't see me do this.' He folded the putty knife and put it back in his pocket.

'Do what?' I said.

A short while later, loitering in the lobby of my own building, waiting for the doors of the freight elevator to open, I heard familiar yapping noises echoing inside the elevator shaft. When the door finally opened, my tall blonde vision was standing eye-to-eye with my cowboy hat.

'Hi, Pyramus, hi, Thisbe,' I said to the yorkie and the maltese. I paused and lit a cigar for dramatic effect. Then I said: 'By the way, I forgot to ask what your name was.'

'Stephanie DuPont. And now I say, "And what's your name?" '

'And now I say "It's Richard Kinky 'Big Dick' Friedman".' I moved into the elevator and took a few puffs on the cigar. 'My close friends call me Fuckball,' I said.

When she was standing safely in the lobby away from the cigar smoke she said: 'I'll just call you Dick.'

'Look,' I said, 'I'm very busy right now, but seeing as we're neighbors and all, why don't you come down sometime. Have a little liquor drink to cut the phlegm.'

She stared at me as if I were an out-patient.

'Banana bread and brie?' I suggested.

'You don't smoke that cigar in your loft, do you... Dick?' I liked the little emphasis she placed on the dick.

'No, of course not,' I said. 'I only smoke in elevators. I'm a thoughtful American.'

'Maybe I'll come down sometime,' she said. 'But *I'll* come down to see *you*. I don't want to walk out of my apartment some day and find you licking my door frame.'

'Don't go giving me ideas,' I said, as the elevator doors closed inexorably between us.

Moments later, still basking in reflected beauty, the cat and I were at my desk like two employees routinely working the dead letter department. Legs had six letters which wasn't bad for a dead man. Of course, most of them were bills.

'Con Ed's gonna have a hell of a time collecting on this one,' I said to the cat.

The cat was not amused. While cats sometimes seem capable of great coldness, not to say cruelty, they have a rather rigid morality when it comes to appreciating attempts at humor about the recently deceased. In fact, cats, to the best of my knowledge, appear to have no sense of humor at all. Unless, of course, you want to count the time the cat took a Nixon in one of Ratso's red antique shoes that had once belonged to a dead man. Ratso was not in the shoe at the time. Neither was the dead man.

'Ah,' I said, as I puffed the cigar and continued the

morbid task, 'an invitation to an opening of what looks like a new and very coochi-poochi-boomalini restaurant.'

The cat looked mildly impressed. Either that, or I'd forgotten to feed her today.

'It says "Coat and tie required". Well, Legs certainly ought to meet that prerequisite. What else have we got here. Ah, a personal letter in a feminine hand.'

I showed the letter to the cat. The cat half closed her eyes, a sure sign of agreement, communication, or, possibly, ennui. It crossed my desk that at this moment there were, very probably, men masturbating in mental hospitals who, in their quite ample spare time, showed letters to cats. This dark thought did not unduly distress me. Many fine and talented people have hung their hats and, occasionally, themselves, in mental hospitals. Van Gogh died in one. Countless Zhivago-like Russians have wasted away in wig city over the years, ending their lives showing letters to cats. Nothing wrong with that. If they'd had mental hospitals in biblical times they'd probably have put Jesus in one and told him he had a Christ complex. Like the Lady of Shalott, I was 'half in love with madness.'

The cat nodded out, but I was still flicking my tail.

I opened the letter.

Reading a personal letter to a dead man is not something you want to do every day. Most of the time it's depressing enough just reading personal letters addressed to yourself.

'Dear Legs,' the letter began.

'It is difficult for me to tell you this but I don't think we should see each other again.'

Great. I took a puff on the cigar and poured a tall shot of Jameson's into the bullhorn. I killed the shot, scanned the letter for any clue to Legs' murder, then placed it under the cigar humidor in the shape of Sherlock Holmes's head. Sherlock himself had said: 'I have never loved.'

Kinky Friedman

Maybe that was the way to go. It was certainly healthier to abstain from love altogether than to try to encourage a rottweiler to hose Dr Watson. There are many who feel that both of the Holmes brothers probably should've been in a mental hospital, along with Jesus, Van Gogh, and the woman who keeps trying to break into David Letterman's house.

I opened the last envelope. Bingo.

It was a receipt signed by somebody at the Joe Franklin Show. It said they'd received the film Legs had sent them and were taking it under review. It said of course he understood the film would not be returned.

'We'll see,' I said.

The cat sat up. Then she opened one conspiratorial green eye. Then she vomited on my desk.

19

'Yes,' said Ratso, with some little pride, 'I have been on the Joe Franklin Show a great many times.' He took a large bite of the big hairy steak on the platter before him.

'In fact,' I said, 'isn't it true that you've appeared on the show more times than anyone else?'

Wooing Ratso by taking him to the Derby Steak House was one of the things you sometimes had to do if you wanted to be a successful little detective. He was close with Joe Franklin and he seemed like he might make a perfect vehicle for goniffing the film. But I had to play my cards carefully.

'That is not technically true,' said Ratso between mouthfuls. 'There are two other people, according to Joe himself, who've been on the show more times than I have.'

64

'You're kidding! Who are they?' I said, exhibiting a good deal more interest in the subject than I felt.

'Guess.'

'Foghorn Leghorn and Ezio Pinhead,' I said, somewhat irritably.

'You're close. It's Georgie Jessel and Otto Preminger.'

'Ah, well.' I tried some of the sliced steak with Colman's hot British mustard. Killer bee.

'Do you think Joe would have you on the show again anytime soon?'

'Well, that's hard to say,' said Ratso, cutting his steak importantly. 'He certainly won't be having Georgie or Otto on anytime soon.'

'Look,' I said, 'I'll put it on a bumper-sticker for you. I think Joe Franklin has a copy of Tom Baker's documentary on Elvis impersonators. I think there must be something in that film that brought about the murder of Legs and Uptown Judy.'

'Jesus,' said Ratso.

'I'll see your Jesus,' I said, 'and raise you a Peter.'

'Well, once they've formally accepted it, a television show will only return something to the party that submitted it.'

'That may be a little difficult in this case,' I said. 'Legs sent the film to Franklin.'

'I'm sure the show's got some kind of policy protecting it that would make it tough for anyone to obtain the film from Joe. Now that Legs and Baker are dead it may soon become very valuable or sought after.'

'It's very sought after right now, numb-nuts. I want that film.' I made a theatrical gesture with my fork toward Ratso. He parried neatly with his knife.

'Look, I can talk to Joe but I doubt if he'll let it go. I wouldn't, in his shoes.'

'Joe's pretty o-l-d. You'll probably be wearing his shoes fairly soon.'

We both took a little sambuca break at this point to calm down and think things over. Ratso adjusted his coonskin cap with the little eyes of the animal pathetically sewn shut. It was not dissimilar to the way many Americans went through their lives, I thought. I'd remember to keep my own orbs wide open just in case anything besides Ratso's steak started to get hairy.

'There is a way you can help,' I said, finally. 'And it'll go a long way toward getting you into the Village Irregulars' Hall of Fame.'

'Whoopee,' said Ratso, with very little discernible enthusiasm.

'You go on the show as a guest and the rest of us will come along as part of that small, informal studio audience he always has. While you're on the show with Joe, his producers and crew – '

' – You'll take the film.'

'Correctimundo.'

Ratso hesitated. Then he said: 'I'll do it. But if Joe finds out I was part of this, I'll never be on the show again.'

'He won't find out,' I said. 'But in the unlikely possibility that he does, at least some good luck will come out of it.'

'What's that?'

'Georgie Jessel and Otto Preminger will finally be able to rest in peace.'

Later that night, Downtown Judy and I strolled the cold, beautiful, half-deserted streets of Little Italy where I could always hear tinny Italian music playing whether it actually was or not. Judy wanted a cappucino, a cannoli, and any new developments that the Village Irregulars had uncovered and, in their petty male chauvinist fashion, hadn't thought to share with her. I wanted about six more sambucas.

'You know, Judy,' I said, as we passed a display of Mussolini T-shirts, 'you should think of it as an honor to be the first woman accepted into an organization that has always been exclusively male.'

'Big fucking deal,' she said.

'That's hardly the spirit.'

'But how can I help if I don't know what's going on?'

'You know everything the rest of us know which, unfortunately, isn't a hell of a lot.'

As we walked, I filled her in on the events of the day, even down to the water blisters on the woman's nose at Uptown Judy's apartment building. As I talked, a clearer picture was emerging in my own mind as well. The Uptown Judy case and the Legs case were hanging together by the merest piece of spit. All they had in common was the eerie way both their places had been torn apart, the fact that they'd both wanted to get in touch with me, and the certainty that they'd both known Tom Baker. It wasn't much but, as I told Judy about the Joe Franklin Show scenario, I knew beyond a doubt that I had to get hold of that missing Elvis film.

'It's not only our best lead,' I said. 'It's our only lead.'

We went to a little coffee shop with outdoor tables even though the night was cold. The building next to it was painted red, white, and green like the Italian flag.

'Did you ever take *her* here?' Judy asked. Even in death, Uptown Judy was making her presence known.

'No,' I said. 'But I imagine her father might've walked with her in these streets when she was a child.'

Downtown Judy shuddered involuntarily.

'Cold?' I asked.

'No,' she said, sipping her cappucino, 'I was just

thinking what it must've been like having a father like
that. Repairing your bicycle in the backyard with all that
blood on his hands and you don't even know it.'

'Fixing your hopscotch games,' I said.

Judy did not laugh. She merely stared down into her
cappucino. I tossed down my sambuca and ordered
another as I chewed thoughtfully on the coffee beans.

'You know,' I said, 'they're both outside of the mortal
equation now. Uptown Judy's gone and her father, Don
Sepulveda, was hit by one of the other families in what
they tried to pass off as a "boating accident" in the Carib-
bean five years ago. Supposedly, there was enough power
behind the explosion to destroy a small city.'

'No one can escape his or her destiny,' said Judy quietly
to the capuccino cup.

'You lives by the watermelon, you dies by the watermelon,' I said.

I drank some more sambuca. If everybody drank enough
sambuca we could probably solve all the major problems
of the world. Religious conflicts and ethnic violence would
no doubt disappear. National boundaries would disinte-
grate and the world would at last realize John Lennon's
dream in the song 'Imagine'. Such is the power of sambuca. Of course, before all this happened, it might be a
good idea, just in case, to buy up a large quantity of coffee
bean futures.

'So you seem to think,' said Judy, 'that Judy was caught
in the same web of the past that finally did in her father.'

'Without a doubt,' I said. 'Regardless of her innocence.
It's very difficult to truly escape the bonds of who you
are. God knows, I've tried by taking Peruvian marching
powder – '

' – Until you had to stop because Bob Marley fell out of

your left nostril,' Judy said, repeating a line of mine in a
rather tiresome impersonation of a Texas drawl.

'I knew drugs weren't the answer. I just had to find out
for myself. As old Slim used to say back on the ranch:
"You gotta find what you like and let it kill you." '

I asked Judy if she'd like to try a sambuca but she
passed. So I ordered myself another sambuca and another
cappucino for 'my lady' as Wayne Newton would've said.

'You don't try sambuca,' I said, 'you stand in the way
of global harmony.' Judy looked at me as if my cowboy
hat had exploded. I was feeling very peaceful and wise
but I could already envision some problems. Sambuca
hangovers causing border skirmishes, civil wars in small
nations, things like that. Maybe the world needed a little
hair of the dog that bit it.

'Well,' said Judy, 'at least I prefer the kind of asshole
you are on sambuca to the kind of asshole you used to be
on the other stuff. Sometimes, even when we were in bed
together, you acted like you didn't even know who you
were with.'

'After cave trip, everybody happy – Burma Shave.'

Downtown Judy made a little moue of distaste. She took
a rather desultory sip of cappucino. I lit a cigar and let the
sambuca do the talking.

'Once, many years ago, when I was in the Peace Corps
in Borneo, I spent several months in a place where so-
called civilized life couldn't touch me. I lived among the
Punan tribesmen, a nomadic group of pygmies who
roamed the dark heart of the jungle eating monkey brains
and killing wild boar with blow pipes. I felt at peace within
the power of their primitivity.

'Once every twenty years or so a western concept
deflected upon this tribe like an errant moonbeam looking
for a lover. Their only contact with western ideas of any

sort had come through the rare interlude with the lost missionary or the rogue mercenary. The only English words that created even a glint of recognition in their brown eyes of innocence were Elvis, Jesus, and Coca-Cola.'

'Elvis, Jesus, and Coca-Cola,' said Downtown Judy.

'Yeah. Sort of a timeless trinity. Like the Old Man, the Boy, and the Spook. I mean, Michael Jackson, Mickey Mouse, and Madonna might be nipping at their heels, but Elvis, Jesus, and Coca-Cola will always be the big three.'

I took another healthy slug of sambuca. Judy stared thoughtfully into the endless Italian night.

'There are, no doubt,' I said, 'other primitive enclaves on this planet, possibly in the outback of Australia, in New Guinea, in the secret hearts of Africa and South America. But these peoples and places are as fragile and ephemeral as a smile in childhood. Yet they do exist. Cultural and spiritual oases where you may truly escape what we have come to think of as the world. Like taking a walk down Yesterday Street. Dancing to music that was written and recorded before you were born. In these places you are safe from harm and sheltered from sorrow.

'If you ever find one of these places, and then leave it, as I have done, you may spend the rest of your life with the better part of your soul living in the shadow of regret.'

Downtown Judy looked across the little table at me with a new-found sparkle in her eyes.

'I'm going with you to the Joe Franklin Show,' she said.

20

The next day was a busy one around 199B Vandam. Ten thousand garbage trucks came grinding through the most hideous hangover I'd ever had in my life.

'To hell with global harmony,' I said to the cat. 'I'll never drink that shit again.' The cat began chasing a cockroach around the loft, leaping from place to place, and doing the whirling dervish routine which was not pleasing to me or my hangover.

I put on my old purple bathrobe and my mental hospital slippers, swallowed about seven St Joseph's baby aspirins from what looked like one of those antique, purple-colored bottles you find at old dump sites, kicked the espresso machine into high gear, and waited for something to happen. At least I ought to get a little buzz, I figured.

The bottle was purple, the robe was purple, the sky was purple, and I was purple. I was also having some pretty unpleasant problems in my gray matter department. I now thought I knew what went on in the mind of an Elvis impersonator.

I poured an espresso and my hands trembled like an alcoholic surgeon's in a B movie. The first sip burned my upper lip rather severely. I put the cup down on the desk and did my best to light a cigar. The lesbian dance class in the loft above me chose this moment to begin a marathon number somewhat reminiscent in length to the choreography in 'They Shoot Horses, Don't They?' I had six million things to do and all I could remember was to feed the cat.

I fed the cat.

The business day began at about 11:45 Jewish Standard Time, when the two red phones on either side of my desk began ringing urgently. I took a few preparatory puffs on my cigar and dumped the ash into the cup which had recently held my third espresso. Cup number four I'd just pour in over the top and drink it ashes and all. I've heard it makes you leap sideways.

I picked up the blower on the left. It was the unmistakable New York-inflected voice of Ratso, which never really sounded right unless it had subway trains and sirens in the background studio mix. This time he had the works going for him including what sounded like a guy breaking up the street with the steam drill that tried to beat John Henry. All the sounds seemed to be emanating from a locus about four inches from Ratso's nose.

'Kinkstah!' shouted Ratso. 'Kinkstah!'

'What hath God wrought?' I said.

'God's wrought me a slot on the Joe Franklin Show! One of the guests suddenly cancelled for tomorrow night!'

'Could you please modulate your voice?' I felt like I'd been recently crucified. Ratso, not quite hearing me correctly, began speaking in a louder, more piercing voice.

'One of the guests suddenly cancelled for tomorrow night!' I briefly held the blower away from my left lobe.

'Did you hear what I said?' shouted Ratso.

'Where the hell are you?' I said, in the barely controlled monotone of a seriously ill person.

'I'm right down the street. I can see your cat in the window.'

I looked to the window and, indeed, the cat did appear to be staring with some distaste at what I could only assume to be either Ratso or a Sonny Bono impersonator.

'Come on over,' I said, 'and bring a large iceberg for my forehead.'

By the time I hung up the blower I was about ready to swoon. I poured a fourth espresso over the cigar ashes and took a healthy slurp. Suddenly, the lesbian dance class went silent. A little man somewhere in my cranium hit a mute button and my headache went away. I took another sip. The sun came out over the city. I felt like the guy who'd discovered penicillin. The absence of pain is a truly wonderful feeling, unless, of course, you happen to be a masochist.

By the time Ratso walked in the door I was wearing a smile almost as big as the one on the puppet head.

'Ratso, my lad,' I said, 'the cat and I welcome you to our airy, spacious loft.' Spacious it may have been, but a thick layer of cigar smoke hung over the place like Mexico City on a bad day and geological formations of unchanged cat litter didn't help the ol' beezer much either. The place smelled as if it couldn't decide whether it wanted to be a hospital or a whorehouse.

'That fucking cat never liked me and never will,' said Ratso. This was undoubtedly true, but the moment called for a diplomatic reply.

'Give her time, Ratso. She'll warm up to you.'

Ratso looked dubiously at the cat. The cat gave him a little mew of distaste.

I poured Ratso an espresso, without cigar ash, and placed him in the chair near the desk.

'I just thought of something,' he said. 'What am I going to do on the Joe Franklin Show?'

'You could pull out your penis like Jim Morrison,' I said.

'Seriously,' said Ratso, as he got up and walked over to the refrigerator, 'the last five times I've been on the show I've talked about my book, *On The Road With Bob Dylan*. Now the producer tells me he wants me to talk about some new project.' Ratso reached into the refrigerator and came out with a to-go order of spare ribs and black bean sauce that had been left over from the Ming Dynasty.

'Well,' I said, 'you can't blame the producer for not wanting a talk show guest who's trapped like an insect in amber.'

'I'll think of something,' said Ratso, as he dug into the culinary artifact with a nearby fork.

'How about "How to Dress for Success?" ' I said.

73

21

After I'd gotten Ratso saddled up and headed north, a rather laborious task, I finally found myself with some time alone to think. I lit a fresh cigar and paced purposefully around the loft a bit. Some fairly cohesive vines were beginning to grow together in my mind. It was time to swing on one of them. I was looking at the Shroud of Turin and I wasn't sure if there was a face on it or not. When I did see the face, it wasn't Jesus. It was Elvis.

I thought about a story McGovern had covered several years before, about a fourteen-year-old girl, a leukemia victim, who'd died somewhere in Kentucky. Her family and the hospital staff were at her side when she died. They were dumbfounded by her last words: 'Here comes Elvis.'

Tom Baker died as he was in the process of finishing a film on Elvis impersonators. Had he wrapped the film before his death? I couldn't ask him. Legs had worked on the film with him as his assistant. Couldn't ask Legs either.

It was well known that the Bakerman had been casual friends with Uptown Judy. His female admirers were legion. Could Tom and Judy have been dancing a good bit closer than anyone suspected? Couldn't ask Tom. Couldn't ask Judy.

Did Judy ever meet Legs? Couldn't ask Judy. Couldn't ask Legs.

There was no evidence of foul play in Baker's death, but then no one was looking for foul play. He was making an Elvis film and had mentioned to Ratso that he was afraid he'd end up meeting Elvis and he did. Legs was helping Baker with the documentary. He ended up meeting Elvis, too. Could either of them have shown the film or talked about the film with Uptown Judy? Even assuming they had, what then? What was it about Elvis or a flock of pathetic impersonators that could set in motion the deaths of three people? Maybe it was far-fetched. Maybe it strained logic. But it was all I had.

I sat down at the desk and laid the cigar gently in the ashtray. I poured a strong portion of Jameson's into the bull horn and poured the bull horn down my neck. I looked at the cat across the darkening, desperate afternoon.

'Here comes Elvis,' I said.

On an impulse, I called the cop shop and, after a fairly interminable wait, got Fox on the blower.

'Tex,' said Fox, 'I'm glad you called.'

'You are?' I said warily.

'Yeah. As you probably know we got a light workload around here and all, and we had a little extra time to go over some of the details of the case of your girlfriend that disappeared. We think we've got a good theory as to what occurred.'

'What's your theory, sergeant?' I said. I lit an old half-smoked cigar and waited.

'Our theory,' said Fox, 'is that she clicked her red boots together three times and went back to Kansas.'

Fox laughed until it sounded like he would choke to death. He recovered, however, and, in a voice that was void of all mirth said: 'Boots are in the property locker. You can pick 'em up.'

'Look, sergeant,' I said, hiding my irritation, 'I don't have a photo of Judy. Did you happen to come up with one I could have?'

'We could get one if we were on the case, but we ain't

on the case. And there were no photos of her in the apartment.'

'You don't find that strange?' I said.

'In this town?' said Fox, and he hung up.

I poured out another shot of Jameson's and with some little pain cast my mind back to the foggy, sordid, almost sepia nights in Uptown Judy's apartment. At least I thought they were sordid. It was hard to tell. It was like dreaming about a dream. But I knew I remembered photographs. Photographs on the table. Shots of Judy in some tropical place. Photos on the dresser. On the book shelves, too, I thought. Framed photographs of Judy and her friends and lovers and family. Of course, I hadn't known that her family was family. But that notwithstanding, it was passingly strange. Could I have been so totally ripped that I was unconsciously transferring the images from one blurry scene to another? The two Judys weren't the only women I'd known in my life and my life at that time was pretty damned out of focus.

No, I thought, the photographs were at Judy's. So? What happened to the pics? The question hung in my mind like a loose thread on an old Elvis scarf. I was still thinking about it when I called McGovern's office at the *Daily News*.

'McGovern World Headquarters,' said McGovern.

'Mit,' I said.

'Mit! Mit! Mit!' said McGovern.

'I need help,' I said. 'I need you to help me find a photo of Uptown Judy. They all seem to have disappeared along with the girl herself. Maybe Brennan can talk to some labs and studios and turn up something. Maybe you can run a piece on her in the paper. Might jar somebody's memory, shake something loose. God knows we need a break.'

'I'll do what I can,' said McGovern, 'but I'm running

the "People Page" these days. Can't put her in unless she was somebody.'

'Christ, McGovern, she *was* somebody.'

'I mean a *socialite* or something,' said McGovern. 'Then I could say "Socialite Disappears Mysteriously". Maybe nothing would come of it but at least my editor'd be happy.'

'Well,' I said, 'she *was* a kind of socialite. She did have sexual intercourse with *me* on several occasions.'

McGovern laughed his loud Irish laugh. I puffed rather self-righteously on my cigar and waited.

'A woman who has sexual intercourse with you can be called many things,' he said. 'But one of them is not a socialite.'

22

I had a little time on my hands so early that evening I walked over to the cop shop and picked up Judy's red cowboy boots. On the way home it started to rain and I carried them under my coat. Now, as they stood up on the counter in my kitchen, I could almost imagine Judy dancing in them. It was hard to believe they'd spooked me so bad the morning I'd found them on my doorstep. Of course, they hadn't walked there themselves. Someone was sending me a message. Judy's dead. Lay off looking for her. It was like some strange force had taken Judy away, removed all traces of her image from the planet, left nothing but a pair of red cowboy boots to say that she was ever here. They seemed small and almost poignant now up there on the counter. Bookends for a life unlived.

These were the somber and mortal thoughts that came to my mind like the heavy gray raindrops to the windows of the loft. It was past time for me to call Tom Baker's dad with some kind of progress report. Somehow the call was difficult to make. Hearing Baker's voice in the voice of his father. Why was this a problem for me? I could already hear Baker's voice in the raindrops.

I figured I'd wait a day or two until after Ratso's appearance on, and hopefully, the film's disappearance from, the Joe Franklin Show. Then, at least, I might have something to report. On the other hand, the unpleasant possibility existed that the receipt Rambam had goniffed from Legs' mailbox was for something else that had nothing to do with Elvis or the Bakerman. In that case there'd be nothing to tell Baker's dad and it'd be time for me to call in the dogs and piss on the fire as we say in Texas.

I poured myself a shot and killed it. The cat slept. The rain fell.

For no reason at all I heard the Bakerman's voice telling me some ridiculous story about a Chinese cab driver he'd had once who, during the course of the ride, found himself strongly desiring to take a Nixon. Baker'd suggested he just stop the cab and go into a restaurant or bar or someplace and he, Baker, would wait for him in the cab. The hack didn't like the idea much and instead took Baker on a route through Chinatown where he finally stopped the cab.

'Must go familiar place,' he'd said.

For some reason Baker had loved that line and repeated it to me many times during the subsequent months rather like an unpleasant mynah bird. 'Must go familiar place, must go familiar place.' Baker, of course, did a pretty good impersonation of the oriental cab driver and seemed to derive an enormous amount of pleasure in irritating me with the repetition of this particular phrase. Back then I sort of swatted it off. Never thought it was very funny. Back then.

I poured another shot and watched the sleeping cat and the falling rain and thought how really humorous the whole notion of Baker harrassing me with this anecdote was. Now that Baker was dead it not only seemed very funny, it almost seemed kind of mystical. I tried it out a few times.

'Must go familiar place,' I said softly so I wouldn't disturb anybody. 'Must go familiar place.' There was something to it all right. It could almost be a mantra for the modern world. Almost. I laughed to myself and repeated the phrase. In my own voice I could hear Baker's voice in whose voice I could hear the Chinese cab driver's voice when suddenly, from the hallway, I heard another voice.

It said: 'Pyramus. Thisbe.'

Then I heard the barking of dogs so small that the sound pierced like the sting of tiny baby scorpions into my gray matter department. This intrusion was followed by several sharp knocks on my door.

I got up and walked over to the door and opened it and Pyramus and Thisbe roared in like two miniature freight trains. The cat woke up from her slumber on the desk and couldn't believe her eyes. I couldn't either when I saw Stephanie DuPont, who'd obviously had a few drinks herself, bringing up a beautiful, languid caboose to the whole situation.

'Come in,' I said to the empty hallway. Then I turned around and saw the cat perched on the edge of the desk like a buzzard on angel dust. Certain death emoted from her eyes as the two little dogs yapped obliviously and traversed rapidly up and down like furry yo-yos in front of the desk. It was a catastrophe waiting to happen. And, sure enough, it did.

The cat, arching her back like a small, land-dwelling dinosaur and making noises that should've frightened any sentient being, had finally had enough. With a particularly well-timed and vicious forehand, she clipped Thisbe just as the little maltese reached the top of one of her piston cycles and sent her crashing into the kitchen counter like a bloody tennis ball.

The barking of the dogs, which, to this point, had been merely unpleasant, now reached a certain crescendo of tedium that taxed both human and feline sensibilities to the limit. Stephanie rushed over to Thisbe and found, apparently, that she was all right. The little dog, indeed, was soon back in her piston rotation in front of the desk.

Stephanie was not pleased by the situation. In a manner not terribly dissimilar to the cat's, she hissed: 'Do something!'

'Can you call the dogs off?' I asked.

'No,' she said, 'but I can call you an asshole. Call your sick cat off.'

This, of course, was not really an option. In as long as mankind has inhabited this weary, star-crossed planet, no one has ever truly called a cat, once committed, off. In fact, no one's ever actually called a cat. Like experienced lovers, they come when they wish.

During the height of all this activity, of course, the phones rang on either side of the three combatants, driving all of them into an almost unimaginable state of frenzy. Picking up either blower would've constituted a hazard to my health so I let them ring. Probably Ratso wanting to brainstorm for subject matter on the Joe Franklin Show. Ah well, there are times in life when all of us have to go it on our own.

After what seemed like the month of Ramadan, things finally began to ease a bit. Stephanie was able to reclaim her two little darlings and cater to their injuries which, thank the Lord, were minor. A dead Thisbe would've made Kinky sexual futures with Stephanie almost unthinkable. It would be fairly long odds as it was.

Stephanie sat down in my desk chair mopping up Thisbe with a warm washcloth. The cat had departed for the bedroom in a rather graceless snit. I knew better than to try to talk to her for at least several hours so I busied myself with being a good little hostesticle.

'Would you care for some banana bread and brie?' I asked Stephanie.

'That sounds nice,' she said.

'Well, I don't have any,' I said. 'How about some Irish Whiskey to cut the phlegm?'

Stephanie nodded sulkily and I poured the drinks into the two most appropriately stemmed vessels I had, a coffee mug and the bull horn. I let Stephanie have the bull horn and told her a little about its history and how I'd acquired such an unusual object. She seemed interested.

'You're the first person I've ever let drink from the bull horn,' I told her truthfully.

'It's grotesque,' she said, holding the bull horn at arm's length. 'If anything happens to Thisbe because of your sick cat I'll sue your ass for everything you own.'

'Well,' I said, 'you'd have to talk to my attorneys about that. They're an old, well-respected firm. Schlemiel, Schlmozzel, and Dealkiller.'

Stephanie smiled fleetingly then began gathering up the dogs, her purse, and one black pump she'd thrown at the cat during the peak of the earlier unpleasantness. The pump had gone wide but I was sure the cat had filed Stephanie's face away in her feline hall of hate which now included almost all living things. I'd filed Stephanie's face away, too. It was so beautiful it was hard to look at directly.

As ol' Rapid Robert once said, you had to just 'shovel a glimpse' every once in a while.

As I was walking her to the door, Stephanie noticed Judy's red cowboy boots on the counter.

'I like those boots,' she said. 'Whose are they?'

'Oh, a friend left them some time ago. She's not coming back. Want to try 'em on?'

Stephanie walked back to my desk chair, sat down, took off her shoes, and waited. I went over to the counter, got the boots, and brought them over to her. She did not make a move to put them on.

'You do it,' she said.

'Okay, Cinderella.'

Though I suspected that most career shoe salesmen were probably sick chickens, I had to admit that it was exciting helping Stephanie DuPont put on those boots. I would've gladly let her keep them if they fit. I was beginning to regard the boots as some kind of albatross or bottle imp anyway, and I'd just as soon they walked out of the loft before they brought more tragedy into my life. I was enough of a shoe salesman, however, to want them to fit.

They didn't. They were too big.

'Jesus,' said Stephanie, 'this whore had big feet.'

As I took the boots off her I noticed they were custom made with the name of the maker inside the boot. That was a lead that needed to be followed and one I should've lamped to long before now.

Stephanie put her own shoes back on and I walked her to the door. I gave her a little kiss on the cheek as she went out carrying Pyramus and Thisbe.

'Stay a while longer,' I said. 'Let's at least exchange phone numbers and hobbies.'

'No, my prince,' she said, 'I have to be home by midnight.'

'Why?' I asked. 'Does your tampax turn into a pumpkin?'

I looked at her and wished, not for the first time, that she'd never leave. She must've seen it in my eyes, for she turned around in the hallway.

'Goodnight, parakeet dick,' she said.

23

Around three o'clock the following afternoon I walked into the green room at the Joe Franklin Show and found a middle-aged psychic studying her tarot cards, a buxom transvestite straightening his pantyhose, and, at a little corner refreshment table, Ratso eating a pizza.

'Nervous?' I asked.

'Hungry,' he said.

In keeping with general green room demeanor, neither of us said much and we kept our voices down to an unnatural level that might've been suitable to a library in wig city. In fact, upon closer scrutiny, the other two occupants of the room looked like they'd just come from hanging out with Van Gogh and Jesus.

'Who goes on first?' I asked Ratso.

'Dame Margot Margot-Howard,' said Ratso, adjusting his dark skyshooters and coonskin cap. I looked at the two other occupants of the room.

'Which one is she?' I said.

Ratso nodded discreetly as he ever did anything toward the guy straightening his pantyhose. Maybe they were long sheer stockings of some kind. I didn't want to look too hard. In my own out-dated quixotic way, I believed there were some things you just weren't supposed to know too much about. I didn't believe in witnessing babies coming out of wombs or seeing the face of the bride before the wedding ceremony. This, very possibly, was the reason I didn't have any brides or babies. Of course, I didn't have any transvestites, either.

'How do I look?' Ratso asked, as he took another slice of pizza out of the box.

He was wearing a pair of red knit pants of some kind and a lox-colored tie, the end of which was very cleverly shaped like a human penis. He had on a cowboy shirt that looked like it might've once belonged to Spade Cooley before he stomped his wife to death in front of the kids.

'Perfect,' I said. 'I especially like the silver collar tips with the little gold square dancing couples on them.'

'Five bucks on Canal Street,' said Ratso with some little pride.

'You're kidding,' I said.

Franklin's studio was in a large television complex situated somewhere deep in the bowels of New Jersey. The three guests on the show appeared well-dressed for the venue. The psychic looked almost like a bag-lady. The transvestite looked almost like an attractive woman. And Ratso, God bless him, looked like Ratso. I was glad there weren't any mirrors in the room or I might've realized that I belonged.

'Know what you're gonna talk about?' I asked Ratso in the lowered voice. Didn't want to disturb anybody who was trying to get a wiggle on.

'Sure,' he said. 'Got it covered.' He reached for another slice of pizza and I took a cigar out of my hunting vest and began my pre-ignition rituals.

I was holding the cigar about a hundred-eighths of an inch above the flame of a kitchen match when my peripheral vision picked up a slight movement over on my left wing. It was the tv, who'd evidently straightened out his pantyhose and was now trying to straighten out me by a prissy little warning gesture with a highly-lacquered finger. I ignored it and him.

'Yoo-hoo,' he said, in an androgynously repellent lilt. 'Smokey The Bear.'

I lit the cigar.

'You get out of here right now with that thing,' shrieked the transvestite, 'or I'll call security.'

'I know you,' I said. 'You were the executive producer of the Howdy Doody Show.'

I left the green room to its rightful occupants. They went back to their slightly nervous little pre-game putterings and I went out into the rather less rarified air of the mundane hallway. I saw a janitor, a secretary, a security guard, a few studio audience types. The folks who'd probably live their whole lives without ever seeing the inside of the green room. I didn't feel too much at home with them either.

I puffed langorously on the cigar for a few moments and then the security guy, always looking for something to justify his existence on the planet, came over and told me to put it out. I did. Didn't want to make a scene. Not quite yet.

I wandered out into the parking lot and, by prearranged plan, waited for various members of our entourage to appear. I lit up a fresh cigar in the fresh New Jersey air and leaned against some kind of nondescript New Jersey motor vehicle. Like everything else in New Jersey it looked weary and rusty and fairly frazzled. It looked like I felt.

I puffed on the cigar and looked around. The view was pretty weak. I'd loitered in finer places than this. But there wasn't any other option. I wanted to go over plans once more with the Village Irregulars before we went into action. At this rate, I was going to miss Dame Margot Margot-Howard.

At about the time I was fresh out of charm everybody showed up. Almost everybody. Mick Brennan, according to McGovern, was hot on a lead. He'd run into a photographer who knew a photographer who'd worked for a time in a lab that had once processed some photos of Uptown Judy.

'How can I put this delicately?' asked McGovern rhetorically. Rambam, Downtown Judy, and I waited.

'Why don't you get to the point?' said Downtown Judy.

'The point,' said McGovern, looking at Downtown Judy, 'is right on top of your head.'

'Look, you two,' I said, 'the altercation is not to occur until Ratso's taping his portion of the show. Hopefully, it'll provide additional cover and distraction so Rambam and I can find what we're looking for. So don't peak too soon.'

'What I'm telling you,' said McGovern, 'is that these photos, that you've set Brennan after, aren't the kind you'd want anybody to know about.'

'Especially your family,' said Rambam. 'With emphasis on the word "family".'

'It's an interesting wrinkle,' I said, 'but it's one we'll have to iron out later. Right now, the Joe Franklin Show must go on.'

We entered the building like typical studio audience types, dulled by life, no sharp edges, ready to let other people get our kicks for us. The security guy in the foyer didn't even look twice at us. It almost hurt my feelings.

Inside the studio, cameras were rolling and Joe Franklin was already talking with Dame Margot Margot-Howard.

Ratso was still most likely in the green room. I hoped he wasn't getting pizza on his penis-shaped tie.

McGovern and Judy took seats near the front and Rambam and I sat down close to the hallway exit. Seating selection was easy since there were only about eighteen people in the studio audience and half of them looked like they were on methadone.

'Robert Frost was right,' I whispered to Rambam.

'He sure was,' said Rambam. 'What'd he say?'

'Hell is a half-filled auditorium.'

It was not precisely clear whether or not Joe Franklin knew that Dame Margot Margot-Howard was a man, but, in a cosmic sense, it didn't really matter. He treated her like a lady. She warmed to the role. She was such a faithful caricature of a society woman that millions of viewers out there in Buttocks, Texas or wherever the hell they were, quite possibly were fooled. The studio audience appeared to care less. As for Joe Franklin, he had his hand on Dame Margot Margot-Howard's shapely knee as she explained that she was head of the Mary Queen of Scots Preservation Society and proceeded to correct many popular misconceptions about Mary Queen of Scots that the viewers in Buttocks, Texas had probably never dreamed of entertaining if, indeed, they'd ever heard of Mary Queen of Scots in the first place.

Dame Margot was explaining how her work as head of the Mary Queen of Scots Preservation Society had led to her writing a book entitled: *I Was a White Slave in Harlem* when I noticed Ratso and the assistant producer entering the studio. This was our cue.

I nodded to Rambam and we slipped out the side door just as Dame Margot was sliding sinuously down the couch closer to the Ed McMahon position and Ratso was depositing himself between her and Joe Franklin. He was on his own now. Flying by Jewish radar.

Rambam and I had our troubles, too. The security guard in the hallway was giving us the old fish-eye.

Rambam walked right up to him. 'Which way's the men's room?' he said.

'I gotta urinate like a racehorse,' I added for good measure. The guard seemed impressed. He pointed down the hall.

I'd covered this territory before earlier in the day. The men's room was around the corner out of sight of the guard unless he came down there looking for trouble. Across from the men's room was the producer's office and next door to it was Joe Franklin's office. We walked down the hall in the general direction of the aforementioned men's room. When we'd rounded the corner I pointed out the two offices to Rambam.

'If I were Baker's film,' I said, 'I'd be in one of those two offices.'

'Let's try door number three,' said Rambam and we went into the men's room. Once inside, Rambam said: 'You take Franklin's office, I'll check the production office. How much time you think we'll have?'

'Depends on how much of a diversion McGovern and Judy can make.' Rambam opened the door very slightly and listened. I could hear the sounds of an altercation coming from down the hallway. Judy's shrill, argumentative tones. McGovern using the 'c' word repeatedly. The guard trying unsuccessfully to keep a lid on things.

'Music to my ears,' I said.

'Cavalry, charge!' said Rambam.

In a nano-second we'd crossed the hall and were in our respective offices. I saw immediately that finding anything in Franklin's office was hopeless. The detritus of a lifetime was piled toward the ceiling like the skyline of a small city suffering from urban blight. More than anything else, it resembled McGovern's apartment. If Baker's film was somewhere in Franklin's office, I was going to have to get the psychic to tell me where it was.

I was starting to admit defeat when Rambam came scurrying into the office holding a large film canister in his hands.

'*Elvis Lives!*' he said, 'Tom Baker. Right on top of the guy's fucking desk. Now we got to find a way to slip it out of here past the tension convention in the hallway.'

It was true that things in the hallway did not sound as if an accord had been reached. The thing seemed to have grown into a major hubbub. I suddenly had an idea.

'Take the film into the dumper, lock yourself into a stall, and wait for me,' I told Rambam.

'Okay,' he said, 'but if you don't come back pretty quick I may start writing graffiti.'

I strode purposefully down the hallway as if I were a busy little television producer myself, but I could've been on a motorized skate board just as well. All the attention in the hall was focused on the security staff and production crew trying with great valor and diplomacy to force McGovern's large Irish body out of the building. I ducked into the green room, smiled at the psychic, grabbed the empty pizza box, and headed back to the dumper.

Moments later, the Bakerman's documentary safely ensconced in the pizza box, and the pizza box firmly in both of Rambam's hands, the two of us headed for the foyer. Rambam had a little Navajo chant going for him even before he got there. He said repeatedly to himself in a loud voice with great concentration: 'They *ordered* pepperoni. I *brought* them pepperoni. They don't *want* pepperoni.'

The security guy smiled at Rambam.

'I'll be back,' said Rambam to the guy.

'That's what my ex-wife told me,' he said.

As we left the building, I noticed a television monitor set into the wall near the front entrance. On the monitor, the Joe Franklin Show was in progress. I stayed long enough to hear Ratso say to Dame Margot Margot-Howard: 'You did say Mary *Queen* of Scots?'

Then I got in a motor vehicle with Rambam and a pizza box containing a friend's final artistic statement. Then I lit a cigar and asked myself once again if a documentary on Elvis impersonators could conceivably create such a trail of doom and destruction.

Life, I reflected, was nevertheless more exciting with a game of chess in it. What you had to watch out for was that sometimes the size of the pieces tended to get rather large.

24

That night, with Uptown Judy's red boots still standing on the kitchen counter and Tom Baker's final cinematic effort still safely ensconced in the pizza box on my desk, the loft seemed to be taking on all the warmth and humanity of a wax museum. Somewhere between the boots of a dead lover and the last crazy creation of a dead best friend, on some metaphysical surveyor's fragile, unworldly plumbline, as yet invisible and unintelligible to mortal man, lay the point called the truth.

I was sitting roughly between the boots and the pizza box, smoking a resurrected cigar, hoping that by mere physical positioning some cosmic awareness might accrue to my weatherbeaten spirit. There had to be a connection somewhere. When I did find it, I had the clear and disturbing feeling it was not going to be the kind of thing you'd want to plug a blow-dryer into.

I turned my attention away from the boots toward the Bakerman's film. I was glad I'd decided to keep it in the pizza box. Stays warm that way.

I had lots of things I needed to do, but now that I had the Elvis impersonator documentary in my possession, I felt a subtle sense of focus and control asserting itself. I needed to keep calm now and think and act rationally.

In the manner of Agatha Christie's great detective, Hercule Poirot, I began straightening objects on the desk, beginning with the pizza box. I worked on that box like Jesse James fastidiously hanging a picture on a wall. It was the last thing Jesse ever did. That dirty little coward Robert Ford shot him in the back just as Jesse's wife was saying 'A little to the right.'

It was as I was straightening other objects on the desk to precise horizontal and vertical positions, that I made a rather disconcerting discovery. The cat had vomited in my pipe.

It was an unpleasant thing to deal with but it was an easy thing to forgive. No doubt, with all the mordant vibes in the loft lately, the cat had become a little nervous, too. I carried the pipe carefully over to the sink, knocked out the vomitus, and ran a little hot water into the little meerschaum bowl that was in all respects an exact replica of the head of President John Fitzgerald Kennedy. Unfortunately, the hole in the pipe where you placed the tobacco was almost precisely in the location of the hole in the President's head created in Dallas, Texas. I finished cleaning the pipe and brought it back to the desk. I didn't agonize over it. I wasn't a conspiracy theorist.

The pipe episode notwithstanding, it was time for one

man to act alone. Namely myself. I had to call Tom Baker's dad. I had to find out any information I could from the place where Uptown Judy had bought the boots. I had to set a bonfire under Brennan's arse to find a photo of Uptown Judy. And lastly, and no doubt most important, I had to arrange for a private screening of Baker's Elvis documentary. Hopefully, it'd provide a clue to whatever the hell was going on. As they say in Hollywood, always eat a pizza when it's hot.

I picked up the blower on the left and called Nick 'Chinga' Chavin who, though he was now a successful ad exec, still had some peripheral ties to nefarious individuals from his days as lead singer with the band Country Porn. As I waited for Chinga to answer I hummed a few bars of the band's hit song, 'Cum Stains on the Pillow (Where Your Sweet Head Used to Be)'.

When Chinga picked up, I explained to him what I needed and, being an ad exec, he quickly grasped the concept.

'When do you need it by?' he asked.

'Yesterday.'

'That's a ball-buster of a deadline but let me see what I can do. You need a place to screen a film in private and it's got to be quick.'

'Correctimundo,' I said.

'I'll do it if it harelips the pope. Call you right back.'

Like most high-ranking executives, Chinga rarely called back when he said he would. I lit a fresh cigar, stoked up the espresso machine and settled in for a wait. About a fortnight later, it seemed, the phones rang.

'Start talkin',' I said.

'I spoke to Charlie Chopbuster. He can get a semi-private screening for you late tomorrow night.'

When Chinga told me the new venue for the screening, I was somewhat credulous.

'Fort Dix?' I said. 'The military base?'

'No,' said Chinga. 'Fort *Dicks*. It's a gay club, but not one of those really seedy ones. You could say it's the cream of the crop.'

'What do you mean by semi-private?' I didn't know exactly what the documentary contained but I did know I didn't want to share it with half of the sentient universe.

'Well, at two o'clock in the morning there won't be hardly anyone in the place. But Charlie can't throw out the few who've paid admission. Anyway, they'll probably be glued to their seats, so to speak.'

'Charming,' I said. I took a few Freudian puffs on the cigar. 'That's the best venue you could get, right?'

'Well, the Helen Hayes Theater was already booked. What're you screening?'

'*The African Queen.*'

'They'll like that at Fort Dicks.'

After I hung up with Chinga I paced the loft a bit and went through a brief round of regret about the choice of Fort Dicks to hold the semi-private screening on the following night. There must be other places in New York where we could screen the film. If I wanted total secrecy I could transfer it to microfilm and hold the screening on the bridge of my nose. At one point in my pacing I began carrying on an animated dialogue with the cat.

'Forget about the pipe,' I said. 'Don't be nervous.'

The cat swished her tail furiously from side to side and her eyes flashed a satanic green.

'Just because the ornaments of death are all around us is not sufficient reason to set us off our nice tuna. Let's work with death if we can. Imagine that we're both unctuous funeral home directors. We come from a well-respected family of feline morticians. Been in the croaking business for generations, passed on from cat to kitten, so to speak.'

Here the cat appeared to display a modicum of interest in the subject. She sat stock still on the counter next to Uptown Judy's boots and stared at me with the intent gaze usually reserved for a cockroach. Possibly, she was watching the pattern of smoke billowing forth from my cigar. Possibly, she was genuinely interested.

'We live and work in a great plantation house with huge white columns in front. Maybe it's in Mobile, Alabama –'

Here, quite abruptly, the cat jumped from the counter to the rocking chair, from there to the sofa, and from there, she scurried rather rudely into the bedroom without a backward glance. Like a great many New Yorkers, the cat had an innate bias against southerners and all things southern. This was most clearly expressed in her absolute refusal to even taste Southern Gourmet Dinner.

I located another dead soldier in the waste basket, poured another espresso and continued pacing the lonely loft into the night. If the path I transversed had been in a straight progression I probably could've walked to Mobile, Alabama. Then where would I be?

I decided it was too late to call Baker's father. Too late in more ways than one. I'd call him after I'd had a chance to see Tom's film. I thought again of calling Chinga back and changing the venue from Fort Dicks to someplace more private and appropriate. But that would only take more time and besides, I didn't want Charlie Chopbuster or his patrons to get the word out in New York circles that I was alarmingly homophobic. Best leave things as they stood. Tomorrow I'd call the Irregulars and invite them down to see the film. I needed every unjaundiced eye I could get. Somewhere in the documentary, I was convinced, might be some clue to the deaths of Uptown Judy,

Legs, and possibly, something to cast the shadow of foul play even upon the death of Baker himself.

Death was in the air, all right. The cat knew it and I knew it and the boots and the pizza carton weren't letting us forget. I wondered what Baker's documentary would be like. Well done, I was sure. All of the Bakerman's work had been clearly chiseled and finely polished. Such a shame he couldn't be here to enjoy it and the subsequent pleasure it might bring to others.

I killed the espresso machine and the lights and put on my old faded sarong. I moved the cat over slightly and got under the covers still pondering the curious relationship between death and art, art and death. I didn't want to end up like Van Gogh, masturbating in a mental hospital, my paintings all stacked neatly somewhere in the attic, unsold and unseen. Sometimes it takes longer than a life. I prayed to St Dymphna that this would not happen.

St Dymphna, as very few psychiatrists but a great many out-patients know, is the patron saint of the insane.

25

The Village Irregulars trooped up to Fort Dicks like parochial children on a field trip to the other side of a dream. And a wet dream, at that. Chinga, curiosity having gotten the best of him, met us at the front of the place.

'Hope you like ammonia,' he said.

'What's an "All-Live Daisy Chain"?' asked Downtown Judy, reading from the marquee.

'That usually happens earlier in the evening,' said Chinga, 'when they have a crowd in here. It's an audience-participation kind of thing. Maybe ten or twelve people'll come up on the stage and join the performers. They take all their clothes off, lie down on the stage, and get in a position with each one's head near the next one's pee-pee. Are you with me?'

Judy nodded her head as if Chinga were explaining photosynthesis.

'No, I'm not, mate,' said Brennan to the empty street. I held the pizza box a little tighter. The film reel had seemed small and vulnerable without the pizza box there to protect it, so I'd brought it along.

'Then they lie there on the stage in a big circle,' said Chinga, 'and simultaneously suck each other's dicks.'

'All the projection rooms in all the cities in the world,' said McGovern, 'and we gotta walk into this one.'

'Let's get it over with,' said Rambam, with a surprising tenseness in his voice.

I was gratified to see the Irregulars turn out en masse for this event. All of them had known Baker to varying degrees and felt, I thought, a sense of personal involvement in seeing this through. Also, they may have correctly assessed the situation: the Elvis film we were about to see had the potential to break the whole case wide open. Even at two o'clock in the morning in front of a seamy, all-male burlesque house the green light at the end of Daisy Buchanan's pier beckoned us onward. Not, of course, to be confused with daisy chain.

Chinga introduced us to the night manager, a sixtyish guy with black leather yachting cap, black leather vest, and black engineer's boots.

'This is Master John,' said Chinga.

'I didn't order a pizza,' said Master John, looking at the package under my arm.

'Let's get it over with,' said Rambam.

The first real wave of ammonia hit us as we walked into the dingy little lobby, faithfully following Master John.

'They wash this place down about every two hours,' said Chinga in a loud whisper.

'Maybe they should go for every hour on the hour,' I said. Ammonia was an interesting thing, I thought. It could erase the smell of sex or death. Yet its very presence, though momentarily fooling the senses, soon came to represent those very things and almost make their impact stronger.

I was surprised to see a popcorn and candy counter with licorice sticks, milk duds, and snicker bars. The popcorn looked like it'd been popped by Orville Redenbacker's grandfather. It seemed somehow unwholesome in a place like this. I was not surprised to see Ratso walk up to the counter and start negotiations with the guy behind it. The guy seemed pretty stale, too.

'Ask him if he's got butterfingers,' Chinga said, in a voice a little louder than necessary.

Moments later we entered the darkened theater.

'The popcorn sucks,' said Ratso.

'So do the customers, mate,' said Brennan.

A second and stronger wave of ammonia hit us as we walked past rows of deserted seats. Here and there, as my eyes adjusted to the tundra-like darkness, were sprinkled occasional patrons – life's little failures – nondescript, gray, excited forms with glasses glinting. On the stage, wearing nothing but a contemptuous smile, was a blond burlesque dancer named Jo-Jo. He was tossing his curls and making his grand exit as our little party took our seats along the third row.

'Best seats I've had on Broadway in years,' said McGovern.

'I went through hell to get 'em,' I said.

'Milk dud?' Ratso asked, offering me the package.

'No thanks,' I said. 'I had an apple on the train.'

97

Chinga signalled me to come with him to give the film reel to Master John to give to the projectionist. Rambam went along with us. On the way up the aisle a young man passed the three of us, then stopped, turned, and made rather serious eye contact with me.

'Everyone loves a cowboy,' said Rambam.

'Except Crazy Horse,' I said.

'He's dead,' said Chinga. 'Unless they try to dig him up and use him as a hand puppet. So what's this big premiere we're gonna be seeing?'

'Tom Baker's documentary on Elvis impersonators,' I said.

'Tom Baker, Movie-maker,' said Chinga. He'd known Baker distantly. Baker'd known a lot of people distantly.

'That's the one,' I said. 'What do you know about Elvis impersonators?'

'I heard they all have little dicks,' said Chinga.

In the lobby a middle-aged guy in a trench coat started staring at my ass. He was close to drooling.

'*Every*one loves a cowboy,' said Rambam.

I took off my hat nervously but soon realized that, because of my kinky moss, my head looked like a rocket ship, and so I put it back on again. All the while, the guy continued to stare at my ass, occasionally licking his lips.

'Unpleasant,' I said.

Rambam shooed the guy away and I gave the reel to Master John who said he'd get it on right away. Charlie Chopbuster was one of Chinga's advertising clients apparently and he'd told Master John to take good care of the straight party that was coming in tonight. Thus, as I turned to walk back into the theater I heard Master John call out to me.

'Look, man,' he said, 'I'm not trying to tell you your

business, but if you keep that brown bandanna in your left hip pocket it means you like to shit on people.'

I thought about it for a moment. While there were some aspects of truth to the sentiment, I felt, in practice, it was giving out a false message. I switched the bandanna to my right hip pocket.

'Look, man,' said Master John. 'That might not be a really good placement idea. Brown bandanna in your right hip pocket means you want someone to shit on you.'

'Well, shit,' I said.

'I'm not into it,' said Master John. He chuckled somewhat in the manner of an old-time children's radio host. I stuffed the brown bandanna deep and out of sight into my coat pocket.

'Now, if it'd been a yellow bandanna – ' said Master John.

'Let's get on with it,' said Rambam.

Master John nodded and headed up to the projection room. The three of us headed back to our seats.

'Christ,' said Chinga, 'how does a 'mo even get to pick his nose?'

'Carefully,' said Rambam.

We took our seats just as the house lights went down.

26

Some years ago, on the left coast of North America, according to a friend of mine who was there, another private screening occurred. It did not take place inside a gay men's burlesque theater, nor did it involve a recently deceased friend's film on Elvis impersonators. Nonetheless, in its own way, it was an equally ill occasion. It was the first private screening of a video to promote the new Michael Jackson doll.

An obscene amount of money had been spent creating this video, apparently, and all the architects and producers of the piece, the best that money could buy, were present in the room.

According to my friend, as the video was being shown, all the top producers and directors who'd put it together were giving a running commentary as the footage rolled. Their comments went something like this:

'Brilliant! Beautiful!'

'Perfectly on target.'

'So accessible.'

'Genius.'

As the video ended there was a brief, almost religious moment of silence. Then a voice from the back of the room could be heard. It was a soft, high-pitched, slightly petulant, bird-like voice. It said: 'I don't *like* it.'

It was Michael Jackson.

Then the Hollywood hot-shots began falling all over each other, tearing their hair, and covering their Armani suits with ashes. Their comments went something like this:

'Christ, what a terrible piece of shit!'

'It's the worst crap I've ever seen in my life!'

'Oh, God, I must've had a nail in my head!'

This little story, which I've since come to refer to as 'The Michael Jackson Anecdote', contains many wonderful lessons in life for all of us. One is: Never underestimate by what a fragile and ridiculous tissue of cat vomit people are attached to their beliefs and convictions in the face of a sickly stage whisper from an androgynous space alien worth twelve billion dollars. The second lesson is more to the point. Whether you're selling Michael Jackson dolls to Third World countries or clearing away the fog on the

moors of several unsolved murders, you must be very
careful to let those helping you form their own opinions.
A chance comment, a reduced cue of some kind, could
lead them off on a wild goose chase. I had fourteen eyes
and fourteen ears and I was determined to use them.

Thus, I made a point of sitting quietly in my seat as the
film began and the voice-over commentary of Tom Baker
rolled across the fetid darkness of the little room like balm
to my soul. In spite of my determination toward total
objectivity and my clinical approach to the project, I found
myself overcome by the voice of my friend.

'Hey, Tom,' I said softly.

McGovern looked over, nodded his head once, and
smiled.

Then, in a darkened porno theater, as millions slept all
around us and dreamed of some day arriving at their
own private Camelots, we seven watched a succession of
shadow men luxuriating each in his own tiny splinter
of light from a distant dead star that would forever be a
hard act to follow.

There were Elvises beyond the imagination. Negro
Elvises, dwarf Elvises, female Elvises, Norwegian Elvises.
There were young fat Elvises, skinny old Elvises, in
between Elvises. There were Elvises that in no physical
way remotely resembled Elvis, yet, in some uncanny after-
image, looked like Elvis. There were Elvises with no voice,
no rhythm, and no talent except the ability to make you
think, if you put your hand over your face and slowly
looked between your fingers, you were seeing Elvis.

There was an Elvis impersonators' convention in Las
Vegas at which the legions of participants were interviewed by the Bakerman. One of the common denomi-
nators was that virtually all of them appeared to be men
of quiet desperation. The Bakerman was non-judgmental.

There was also the mandatory pilgrimage to Graceland, Elvis's home in Memphis. The impersonators, descending upon the place like eager locusts, tended to lose whatever star appeal they may have had the closer they got to the King's home. At Graceland, possibly not surprisingly, they went through empty postures and rote mannerisms but clearly emerged as what they truly were – fans. Fans with a curious admixture of love, passion, envy, anger, and beneath that, some arcane form of self-doubt, and what almost seemed to be clinically ill self-loathing. In other words, they were just like the rest of us.

Through all of this, like the muddy, winding river of life, travelled Tom Baker's resonant Irish voice – seeking, encouraging, comforting. In the dark burlesque house, I momentarily stripped away the Elvis impersonators and communed with that disembodied voice I knew so well. I'd taken for granted that it would always be with me. Now, I felt a great inner peace, as if I'd died and gone to the Baby Jesus or Buddha or L. Ron Hubbard and then suddenly realized they were all in attendance at the same AA meeting in the sky. It was almost a mystical experience for me – almost as if I'd been working out for an hour and a half on my Thigh-Master – but it wasn't helping me find out who killed Uptown Judy or who croaked Legs.

Suddenly, a large, dark, muscular figure leapt to the stage. Because of the pose he struck, at first, I had him lamped for an over-zealous Elvis impersonator. All he was wearing was a codpiece about the size of Moshe Dayan's eye-patch. It looked like it had a Volkswagen double-parked behind it. Nonetheless, the man was strikingly handsome, and not without a certain effortless Latin charm as he began giving *lambada* lessons to the sparsely popu-lated room.

'And step, step, step. And step, step, step,' said the man.

The Elvis impersonators gyrated obliviously behind him on the screen, their hips undulating in a fashion not dissimilar to his own.

I looked at our small group of theater-goers. Ratso, Rambam, Brennan, and McGovern were all convulsing with laughter. Judy looked like she'd been hit with a piledriver. And Chinga, turned fully toward the projectionist, was shouting: 'Stop the film! Stop the film!'

'And step, step, step,' said the man. 'And hip, grind, THRUST!' He was becoming increasingly animated even as the film froze behind him.

Chinga grabbed me now and spoke very fiercely and intensely close to my ear. He said: 'Look, I've been in advertising long enough to know what doesn't belong in a picture. I don't look at what the magician wants me to see.'

'Pivot, lunge, and dip!' shouted the *lambada* instructor, performing the insane motions alone on the stage.

'I notice the car that somehow sneaks into the frame in the commercial of the Old West,' Chinga hissed.

At this point, the male dancer leapt off the stage and grabbed the person seated closest to him. It was Ratso. Ratso's drink spilled all over him and the popcorn and milk duds went flying.

'There was something very familiar in that last segment,' Chinga continued. 'Where the Elvis impersonator was singing in that Italian restaurant.'

The next thing I knew, the guy had Ratso in an iron grip, pulling him tightly against his practically naked, heavily sweating body. We all stood up to get a closer look at the couple doing the *lambada* on the dance floor.

'Loosen your hips!' the guy shouted to Ratso. 'Follow my lead!'

' "I saw a man dance with his wife," ' sang McGovern.

'Don't look at your feet,' the guy told Ratso. 'Look in my eyes.'

Eventually calm was restored, and everything in the little theater went back to merely sordid. A much-relieved, out-of-breath Ratso returned to his seat as Master John very apologetically hustled the guy out of there. I gave Ratso my brown bandanna to wipe his sweater. Chinga signaled the projectionist. The film rolled again.

What we saw now was some footage of an Elvis impersonator performing before some tables of old men in what looked like an old Italian restaurant. Baker's voice-over was saying: 'We traveled all the way to Sheepshead Bay, Brooklyn to catch this next pretender to the throne.'

Chinga stood up and shouted: 'Stop! Stop the film!'

We all saw it at the same time. It *was* a familiar face.

Sitting at a corner table in the background, sipping an espresso and smiling blandly, was Don Sepulveda.

27

It was four-thirty in the morning and only paranoia was keeping us awake. Rambam had driven me, Ratso, and Mick Brennan back to the loft for coffee and cordials and the four of us along with the prodigal pizza carton were now squeezed into the freight elevator too tightly to even look at our shoes.

'You think anybody there besides our little party saw Sepulveda in the film?' Ratso asked.

'Doubt it,' said Brennan. 'Everyone'd left by then and Master John was out in the lobby probably inspecting handkerchiefs or something.'

'What about the guy showing the film?' Ratso said.

'He didn't see a thing,' said Rambam. 'That little skell was running on eleven different kinds of herbs and spices.'

'My dear Ratso,' I said, 'you're projecting your paranoia on the projectionist.'

Though I didn't say it, I shared Ratso's concern. Judy had left Fort Dicks in a semi-snit and McGovern and Chinga both had pleaded heavy workloads in the morning and had gone home, too. But the seven of us – the Village Irregulars – now shared a dark and potentially quite dangerous secret. Don Sepulveda was alive and well – not rubbed out five years ago as the world had thought. Every top fed and mafia boss would've probably let you lay your dick on his wisdom tooth for this information. Not that that was a particularly attractive offer.

If you thought about it, it got so spooky it almost didn't seem real. So I tried not to think about it as the four of us entered the loft. I casually flipped the pizza box onto the desk and walked over to the kitchen cabinet and got out a bottle of Bushmills for the group. Had to entertain the guests and down deep, I suppose, I could use a drink myself.

'Just give me an espresso,' said Rambam. 'I've got a stake-out in Quogue, Long Island.'

'You can't have a stake-out in Quogue, Long Island,' said Ratso. 'It's a contradiction in terms. There's nothing there to stake out.'

I started the espresso machine and lit a cigar. Brennan poured drinks for Ratso and myself and an extremely hefty shot for himself.

'Well, it's kind of funny,' said Rambam. 'This old woman in Quogue, Long Island lost her cat and I did a door-to-door to try and find it. I found another old lady who had a lot of cats and reported that every morning around 6 a.m. a cat matching the description comes into her yard and tries to fuck one of her cats.'

'Are you giving her statement verbatim?' asked Brennan.

'Close,' said Rambam. 'Anyway, so I'm going out tonight to try to catch the cat in the act and bring him back to his owner.'

'Well,' I said, 'I can see why you'd want to go out to Quogue, Long Island and try to get that cat back for that lady. All we got here's a couple of murders and a little don that's popped up after five years.'

'The difference is,' said Rambam, pausing rather dramatically to blow on his espresso, 'that woman's paying me and you're not.'

'I'll drink to that,' said Brennan, 'we ought to get hazard pay.'

I killed my shot and took a few disbelieving puffs on the cigar.

'What's happened to you guys?' I said. 'What's happened to the fabled Village Irregulars?'

Ratso replied in a high-pitched Sly Stone inflection. 'Who *you*?' he said. 'What you *do*?'

After a tense moment or two, everyone laughed and Rambam put his large hand on my shoulder.

'Don't worry,' he said. 'Tomorrow we'll get on the track of the bad guys again. I think I know where that restaurant is in Sheepshead Bay. You and I can go out there tomorrow afternoon and talk to some people. Or we could just send Ratso.'

'Sure,' said Ratso. 'You can look for me on the third star to the left.'

'No,' I said, 'I've got something else in mind for Ratso.'

'I can hardly fucking wait,' he said.

'I can't wait either,' said Rambam. 'Got to get to the

stake-out. By the way, I've checked with the DMV – that's Department of Motor Vehicles to you – and we could have a photo of Uptown Judy soon.'

'What's soon?' I asked. Brennan's interest perked up now.

'About three weeks,' said Rambam as he headed for the door.

'Three weeks!' said Ratso. 'I still remember the shadow of Sepulveda's smile. He finds out we're onto him, we could all get rubbed out.'

'There's another reason for going out to Quogue, Long Island,' said Rambam, as he walked out the door.

After Rambam had taken his leave, the three of us had another round of Bushmills in silence. It was hard for me to believe that the closest to an establishment type that we had among us was Rambam. Maybe we were in deeper shit than I thought.

'Here's something you may need,' said Ratso. He threw my brown bandanna in the direction of the desk. It happened to land directly on top of the pizza carton.

'Cosmic,' I said.

'Now that our friendly neighborhood P.I. has left the premises,' said Brennan, 'I think I may come up with a photo a lot faster than three weeks. But things could get a little weird.'

'What do you mean "get"?' said Ratso.

'Snuff films,' said Brennan. 'I'm on the track of a guy rumoured – only rumoured – to've made a few. I've heard he might've done some sessions with Uptown Judy.'

I felt a little chill in the room. I looked over at the cat who was sleeping in kind of a half-moon position. They say you can tell by how tight a ball a cat rolls itself up in just how cold it is. Of course, this doesn't allow for the perversity of cats, who might roll themselves up into a very tight ball just to make you think it's cold. It also doesn't allow for the perversity of the weather. Otherwise, it's a pretty good indicator.

'Who is the guy?' I said.

'I don't have a name or face yet,' said Brennan, 'but I'm working on it. I've talked to burned-out hippie models from the seventies, escort service girls, porno stars. It's coming together. Newspaper morgues have been pretty helpful.'

'Couldn't McGovern help you with that?' asked Ratso.

'Reporters are just chimpanzees at typewriters,' said Brennan. 'They just never quite understand the inner workings of the photographic mind.'

The photographer's bias against reporters aside, Brennan sounded like he was clearly onto something. All I needed, I thought, was yet another possible scenario for Judy's disappearance. Was her death connected directly to Tom Baker's film? Was it a mob hit? Could a snuff film-maker have used Uptown Judy as his leading lady? Maybe she did click her red boots together three times and go back to Kansas.

Without thinking I let my hand gently graze over the red cowboy boots on the counter. Ratso observed this, apparently, and his penchant for dead person's shoes must've kicked in.

He said: 'Those were hers? Can I try 'em on?'

'Well,' I said, 'it's not a request we get every day from gentlemen callers but why not?'

'They are moderately uni-sexual,' said Brennan, no doubt trying to ease the embarrassment both of us felt.

Ratso set down his drink and picked the boots up off the counter. He had a lot of dead people's shoes and clothing and, no doubt, he was already visualizing the boots standing in a place of honor in the clutter of his closet floor. He walked over to the chair by the desk to try them on. I turned away from the rather obscene spectacle and poured myself another shot of Bushmills. I killed the shot and tried not to listen to the gruntings and rantings of Ratso as he forced his feet into the boots. I poured out another shot for both myself and Mick Brennan and we made a little cocktail chatter to compete with a noise that sounded like the Stoney Mountain Cloggers live from the Grand Ole Opry.

When I turned around again Ratso was already back in the chair trying, rather unsuccessfully, to get the boots off. I could see that they were several sizes too small and it was not going to be easy. He was clearly in some pain.

'Motherfucker!' he shouted.

'As a fellow American,' I said, 'let me help you take them off.'

Eventually, the feat was accomplished, and the feet which remained on the floor of my loft, clad in green socks with little red hockey players, seemed quite relieved.

Ratso leaned back in the chair like a dead man. After a long interval, he spoke in a wistful mock-tragic tone.

He said: 'Sometimes I wonder if I'll *ever* find my Prince Charming.'

'Mate,' said Brennan. 'Have you tried Fort Dicks?'

28

The morning broke cold and lonely over the city, almost as if it knew I was going to call Tom Baker's father. Possibly the problem for me was that finding the film had become almost a spiritual task. Now that I'd found it I had to admit that Tom Baker was really dead. If it can be said that crazy Irishmen ever die. Personally, I doubt it. I think they come back like the green buds of springtime, leprechauns bringing courage and irrational cheer to the loneliest moments of all our lonely lives.

'Mr Baker,' I said. 'It's Kinky in New York.'

'I know,' said Tom Baker's father. 'It's kinky out here in San Francisco, too.'

The apple never fell far from the tree, I thought. Of course, as Allen Ginsberg once reminded me, 'Sometimes the tree falls down.'

'We've found Tom's movie,' I said.

'That's great news, Kinky. I got a call a few days ago from a woman who's Joe Franklin's secretary. She said the film had been stolen and wondered if I had a copy. Of course I didn't.'

'Like I said, we've got the film. I'll have a copy made and send you the original as soon as I check out a few things.'

'That's wonderful. Tom was very proud of his work.'

'I'm proud of Tom's work, too,' I said.

'We've put Tom's ashes on the Embarcadero. You know he grew up there. Played there as a kid.'

We talked a while longer, promised to keep in close touch, then we hung up and I walked over to the kitchen window. The cat jumped up on the sill and stood next to me. I stroked her gently until her purring seemed to rise above the noise of the street and fill the loft with something akin to peace of mind. I wasn't sure whose mind. It almost didn't matter.

I didn't know what the Embarcadero looked like but I hoped to hell it wasn't as drab as Vandam Street that morning. I knew it was somewhere by the ocean. Probably a beautiful view. Pick up a sea breeze every now and then. A little sunshine. A little rain.

'Must go familiar place,' I said to the cat.
The cat said nothing. But her eyes were green.

29

Most people who live in Manhattan are about as likely to visit Khazakstan as they are to ever go to Brooklyn. This does not necessarily reflect negatively upon Brooklyn. It just shows how small-town big-city people are. Rambam, of course, lived in Brooklyn, and was probably one of the reasons people in Manhattan didn't like to go there. Nonetheless, later that morning, I found myself arguing with him on the blower, in favour of making the trip.

'Let's go on out there to that restaurant,' I said. 'Soak up some ambience. After all, if we can find where the Don Sepulveda sighting took place, something may start to happen.'

'We can find it all right,' said Rambam. 'And something no doubt will start to happen. But it'd be safer if we use the old hardboiled computer method.'

'What is the old hardboiled computer method?'

'We access wire transfers from the bank. Say a hundred credit cards used that night the Elvis impersonator was there. Find a guy in his fifties with a credit history of only a couple years. Could be our man.'

'What if he paid cash?'

'We're fucked.'

'Look, let's use the old Sam Spade approach. Let's go to the fair and see the bear. No computer ever devised knows how to follow a hunch.'

'And I was so looking forward to cross-referencing databases.'

And so it was that I found myself looking out over the

fishing boats on Sheepshead Bay and wondering what our own catch would be by the end of the afternoon. Off to the right were the bay and the fishing fleet, and on the left were lobster restaurants, clam joints, and old men who looked like Don Sepulveda impersonators drinking espresso at outdoor tables.

'Those guys must have iron balls,' I said.

'They go inside when it snows,' said Rambam. He slowed the car a bit and seemed to be looking for the place by Italian radar.

'Why do they call this Sheepshead Bay?' I asked. 'Some guy wake up one morning with a sheep's head in bed next to him?'

'Nothing that exciting. Several hundred years ago there used to be a sheep *shed* here and over the years the name became perverted.'

'So did everybody in New York,' I said.

It didn't take Rambam long to park the car and point across the way to a certain restaurant.

'How do you know that's the place?' I said. 'They all look the same.'

'Not to an Italian.'

'What do we do now?' The place suddenly did not look all that inviting.

'We go in, order an espresso, drop a name, and hope it's the right one.'

'Maybe we should first try cross-referencing some databases.'

Rambam got out of the car. 'Let's go, Sam Spade,' he said.

We went in, ordered two espressos, and struck up a rather lifeless conversation with the only thing who seemed to be moving in the place, a heavy-set, tough-looking guy named Dominick. Obviously, the name

Rambam dropped has been changed to protect both of our asses, but the pertinent conversation, as I heard it, went something like this:

Rambam: 'You know, I'm a friend of Frankie Lasagna's. If you'd help us out I think he'd really appreciate it.'

Dominick: 'I don't know nuttin'.'

Rambam: 'That time you had that Elvis impersonator down here, that must've been a wild night.'

Dominick: 'You want a cannoli with that?'

Rambam: 'No thanks. You guys use a mailing list or anything for that Elvis impersonator show?'

Dominick: 'I don't know nuttin'.'

Rambam: 'Look, I'm just doing a favor for Frankie Lasagna. Can we have a look at the credit card stubs for that night?'

Dominick: 'I don't know nuttin'.'

At this point, Dominick glowered at us and walked away through a door in the kitchen.

'That Frankie Lasagna name really opens the doors, doesn't it,' I said. I lit a cigar and took a few puffs to settle my nerves.

'Watch that kitchen door,' said Rambam. 'When it opens he's either going to be carrying two espressos or an uzi.'

'Too bad we didn't have a meal here. It'd be a nice digestive aid.'

'I tell you, Frankie Lasagna should've worked.'

'Maybe he don't know nuttin',' I said.

Moments later, the kitchen door opened and Dominick came out with two espressos and a scowl. We drank the espressos. I smoked the cigar.

As we went over to pay the check, Rambam took out a card and wrote a number on it.

'If you decide to know something,' he said, 'give me a call.'

We left the place and walked to the car without looking back.

'I don't think he knows anything,' said Rambam.

'He made that pretty clear,' I said. 'But doesn't this make you kind of nervous?'

'Why should I be nervous?' said Rambam. 'I gave him your phone number.'

30

I didn't sleep very well that night. I dreamed that Dominick was holding me at gunpoint with some large unpleasant Wyatt Earp kind of handgun. Dominick was smoking a cigar and, to make things more painful for me, a slower death, he kept one end of the cigar in his mouth and the other, the lit end, held against the hammer mechanism of the gun. He was waiting for it to get hot enough to explode and kill me and I was becoming quite agitated waiting for a pizza to be delivered.

'I *ordered* pepperoni,' I said, 'I expect them to *bring* me pepperoni.'

'I'm sure I don't know a thing about this matter,' said Dominick in a highly cultivated British accent.

The pizza in the dream finally arrived. It was brought to me by Uptown Judy. There was a black funeral wreath on top of the pizza box. She was wearing her red cowboy boots.

'Nice boots,' I said.

'I need them,' she said. 'I'm headin' for the last round-up.'

There were some important questions I knew I wanted to ask her, but, in the irritating fashion of dreams, I could not put the right words together. All I could do was keep repeating my petulant little pepperoni monologue and watch Dominick puff away on his cigar.

'Why you lookin' at me,' he said, vaselining back to his Italian persona. 'I don't know nuttin'.'

'But I do,' said Uptown Judy, and she opened the pizza box.

Her flesh began melting.

'How're you gonna find me,' she said in a voice that was fading with the dream. 'How're you gonna find me if you don't know who I am?'

Some of her flesh, I noticed, was now falling directly onto the pizza in rather neat little circles that bore an uncanny resemblance to pepperoni. Her eyes fell somewhere into the pizza like two olives and I found, as I stared into their empty sockets, that I could no longer remember if they were green or they were blue or if they merely resembled Elton John's. As the dream ended, I heard a dull explosion somewhere in the near distance and woke up to find the circulation to my scrotum rather severely restricted by an unfortunate twist in my sarong.

I stumbled out of bed, rectified the situation, and noticed that the cat had knocked one of Judy's red cowboy boots off the counter, no doubt causing the muffled explosion at the end of the dream. There's a lot of reality in our dreams. Fortunately, we manage to sleep through most of it. There's also a great deal of dream material in our lives. Fortunately, we manage to live through most of it.

Just at the moment things looked black indeed for myself and the cat. In my case, I was out of espresso. In my maddening search for the cabinets and drawers in the kitchen, some of them having not been opened in many years, all I found was a small jar of decaffeinated instant, left there long ago, no doubt, by some forgotten lover. I always have believed that if you drink enough instant decaff you will cease to exist.

The cat's situation was equally precarious. She was obviously very hungry and all she had left was one can of cat food. Southern Gourmet Dinner.

To add to our problems the phones began ringing rather ominously. I walked over to the desk and picked up the blower on the left.

'Dis is Dominick,' said the voice.

'Yeah,' I said. This couldn't be happening so soon after my dream.

'Me and da boys're comin' over – '

'That's very cute, Rambam.'

'There's as much chance of him calling as there is of Jesus coming back in a Studebaker.'

'How about a Christler?' I quipped, quite elated to have escaped mob vengeance for another day.

'Look, I'm working on the hardboiled computer approach, but if this guy faked his own death successfully he's too smart to fall into some credit history trap. He's probably got a string of false identities that'd reach from Vandam Street to Sheepshead Bay.'

'There's a route I won't be taking again.'

'You won't have to,' said Rambam. 'I think the solution to your little problem lies much closer to home. You don't know much about Uptown Judy. You don't know what she was really all about. You didn't even know her dad was a big-time mobster. You want to find what happened to her you've got to fill in her background more fully. I can't believe you were hosing somebody and you don't really know a fucking thing about her.'

'Okay, so I was slightly amphibious,' I protested. 'I didn't even know who I was. How the hell am I supposed to remember who she was.'

'Well, that's what you've got to find out. You got the Elvis documentary back for Baker's dad. You correctly connected Uptown Judy with the film. But now you're in deeper waters. Not just doing a favor for a dead friend's family. You're investigating two murders. Because you don't know shit about the victims – the first thing every good investigator tries to learn – you're all over the road. You can't get a focus on things. You really got no case at all until you find out more about who was this person you call Uptown Judy.'

Having the attention span of a cocker spaniel, it was one of the longest incoming wounded monologues I'd listened to in years without interrupting. Of course, I was fairly brain-dead at the time because of the espresso situation. But I was very glad I'd listened.

'Thanks,' I said. 'You've really put the thing in perspective for me.' Even if he'd spent the previous morning on a cat stake-out, I knew Rambam was making sense.

'Forget it,' he said. 'You're handling a tricky case here. My gut feeling – my Jewish-Italian intuition – tells me that these two murders could well have been connected but they probably weren't done by the mob.'

'I'll be sure and tell that to Dominick when he calls,' I said.

'He's not gonna call,' said Rambam. 'Whether or not this case gets solved is going to depend on only one thing.'

'And what would that be?' I asked. I lit a cigar and waited but I still wasn't ready for Rambam's reply when it came.

'How many brain cells you haven't fried,' he said.

After I cradled the blower I sat at the desk for a long while in the manner of your everyday catatonic. My mind was humming along on about one cylinder. I knew Rambam was right. In the final analysis it would devolve to me to solve this case. The Village Irregulars, invaluable as they often were, could only clearly see the parts of the puzzle that had been delegated to each of them. If anybody could see the whole picture, it ought to be me. Good luck, I thought. At the moment I had my hands full coordinating the motor control to relight my cigar.

Finally, I gave up the task, put the cigar in the ashtray, picked up the cat, and, still in my brain-dead state, walked over to the couch for a little power nap. I'd only been awake for about half an hour but it'd been very taxing. Already there appeared to be some leakage between the pizza dream and the Rambam phone call. They were starting to run together like my old tie-dyed pair of socks.

I laid down on the couch with the cat on my chest and tried to imagine Uptown Judy's face. It was a blank like Inspector Maigret's. For a moment, I thought I had something. Something familiar in a smile, in the eyes. Then I lost it – thanks largely to the nightmare whirlwind of drugs, booze and fast-lane insanity that at one time I called my life.

I kept mixing Uptown Judy in with all the others and losing her in dark, disembodied images percolating up from someplace in my not-so-distant past. It was the kind of thing that, providing you were sane at the moment, could drive you crazy.

At least I knew Maigret's habits and mannerisms and style – could see him smoking his pipe, could see his raincoat hanging up by the radiator, could see him familiarizing himself with the victim of the case, patiently, passionately, ruthlessly, almost as one would with a lover.

' "How do I love thee," ' I said to the cat. ' "Let me count the ways." '

31

'Hell no,' I said to Downtown Judy, 'we don't need your help locating Don Sepulveda. We're already on his trail, it's too dangerous for womenfolk, and, besides, you've interrupted my power nap.'

'But I want to help,' she said plaintively. I held the blower in one hand and lit a post-power-nap cigar with the other.

'To quote my friend Chinga: "A woman's place is on my face," ' I said stolidly. 'The mob already has my number, Judy. I don't want them to get yours.'

'Wait a minute,' she said. 'I'm supposed to be told as much about the case as the other guys. I thought this was the Village Irregulars. All for one and one for all!'

'Fuck the Village Irregulars,' I said, 'and feed 'em Froot Loops.'

'Fuck you!' said Judy, her voice breaking with emotion.

'All right, look,' I said. 'You could help Brennan track down his crazy story about the guy with the illustrious past in the snuff film industry. Supposedly, according to lowly-placed sources, he may also have some photos of Uptown Judy which we badly need to circulate and which I badly need to jump-start my memory bank. Right now, the times I was with her seem almost like a dream. Maybe she wanted it that way.'

There was silence on the line and I wondered briefly if jealousy was again rearing its ugly green head.

Then Judy said: 'What's a snuff film?'

Oh Christ, I thought, we're sending a lamb to the slaughter. Nonetheless, it seemed at the time to be safer for Judy to be helping Brennan run down a rumour about a snuff film-maker than to be stumbling around the trail of a desperate mafia don with Pelligrino in his veins.

'A snuff film,' I said, 'is an illegal, amoral actual cinematic documentation of a person getting croaked. An actor has to really be desperate to take the job. There are of course, no sequels.'

'Jesus,' said Judy. 'Have you ever seen one?'

'No, but I've seen a lot of performances that have made me wish the movie was a snuff film.'

'And this guy may have photos of Uptown Judy?'

'Yes. And he may be very dangerous to children and green plants. If you locate him or his studio don't mess with him. Call me.'

I gave Judy Brennan's phone number, told her to work closely with Mick, and warned her again that if they should miraculously find the monster, not to approach it. She was almost in a state of sexual excitement when I hung up the phone. I was not in a state of sexual excitement when I picked up the blower again and called Ratso.

'Can you meet me at the Garden in a few hours?' I said.

'The Garden?'

'You know, the place you go about 79 times a week to watch hockey. I want you to take me through that rat maze, pardon the expression, so we can talk to a few of Uptown Judy's employers or co-workers.'

'Okay,' said Ratso, 'but the meter's running. This'll cost you at least one more big hairy steak.'

'Done,' I said.

'Medium-rare,' said Ratso. 'By the way, I've found out some interesting shit about Elvis. Did you know they now believe Elvis was Jewish?'

'That's funny,' I said. 'He didn't look Jewish.'

I cradled the blower, picked up a few cigars, and told

the cat she was in charge of the boots, the pizza box, and the loft while I was gone. I put on my cowboy hat and hunting vest and stepped into a half-frozen, steel-gray afternoon. Nobody had their picnic basket out. A guy living in a cardboard box down the street was cutting little windows out of the sides like you used to do when you were a kid. If anybody was ever a kid.

I walked to Seventh Avenue to a little deli-grocery store run by some kind of born-again Koreans. More and more I was beginning to believe that I had the soul of a Korean businessman. I did not waste time on the window dressing of life. I survived only on the bare essentials. And these I stockpiled fairly heavily. If things got much worse in the city I might not want to go out again.

I bought enough cat food for all nine lives, enough cat litter to accommodate a snow leopard if any still existed, and enough espresso to keep Little Italy awake past its bedtime which is never. I also made a fairly sizable investment in toilet paper.

As I lugged my purchases up Vandam Street, my thoughts were not on meeting Ratso at the Garden. Or on Judy and Mick and the snuff film character. Or on Rambam cross-referencing databases. Or on the whereabouts of Don Sepulveda. Or on Elvis impersonators. Not even on my own horror at how the Swiss cheese effect had hamstrung my mind to where I could barely recall a woman I'd been to bed with.

My thoughts instead were of a bright vivid long-ago summer day on our ranch in Texas. I'd gone into the storeroom and come out with three rolls of toilet paper. My friend Slim sitting on a wooden Coke crate, leaning against the dining hall and drinking a can of warm Jax, his old black sun-blinded face under a paper Rainbow Bread cap watching the world go by. As I emerged from the storeroom carrying the three rolls of toilet paper, Slim had made a comment that I have never forgotten and one that has been a guiding spiritual force through many of my life's darkest hours.

'How many assholes you got?' he'd said.

32

Several hours later, Ratso and I met at the Will Call window of Madison Square Garden. We'd met there many times before but this particular afternoon it was not to get tickets to a Ranger game. This was not a game. We weren't going into the Garden. Instead, we walked to a nearby building called 4 Penn Plaza which housed the Garden's executive offices. We signed in, rode elevators, talked to receptionists, all the things that little people usually do in big skyscrapers.

After two-and-a-half hours of listening to Ratso wheedle, worm, charm, and cajole his way into practically every office remotely related to the activities of the Garden, an interesting pattern emerged. No one had ever heard of Judy Sepulveda. At the public relations office where I was under the impression Judy had worked, a three-thousand-year-old woman trotted out her computer to show that no one named Judy had ever held a full-time position there. Much less Sepulveda. But it did seem to ring a distant bell to her. Maybe she'd heard it somewhere else.

As we left the building and decided to walk a few blocks down Seventh Avenue, Ratso commented that he was surprised I was in such an upbeat mood.

'Finally,' I said, 'after two-and-a-half hours of hell I'm able to light a cigar without some hemorrhoid-ridden nerd in a monkey suit telling me to put it out.'

'You got an extra cigar?' said Ratso.

'They don't make 'em extra,' I said, but I fished one out of my coat pocket and handed it to Ratso who then borrowed my butt-cutter, my matches, and my last nerve.

'C'mon,' said Ratso. 'You're in a good mood. You're not disappointed. It's like you expected this. What's up?'

'I'm just filled with admiration for you. I knew you were good but I didn't know you had a PhD in name-dropping.'

Ratso looked slightly hurt. 'I wasn't name-dropping,' he said. 'I just know a lot of people who know a lot of people.'

I smiled at Ratso as we walked up Seventh, puffing on our cigars, vaguely enjoying the ever-changing human scenery.

'And none of whom,' I said, 'seem to know Uptown Judy.'

Ratso claimed he still had some work to do at the *Lampoon*, so after another block or two, he grabbed a cab and I continued walking toward the Village. For a while now something had been tickling at the back of my mind and, finding that Uptown Judy had apparently fabricated her job at the Garden, turned the tickle into a shower massage of my medulla oblongata. It was a veritable symphony of wrong notes. I couldn't name the work or the composer yet, but it was most assuredly a virtuoso performance.

I walked all the way back to the Village to clear my head and then, when that didn't work, I stopped at a little Irish bar to mess it up again. When I got to the loft it was ten o'clock and I didn't know where my children were. I wasn't even sure what had happened to my imaginary childhood friends.

I made a little small talk with the cat and a little before bedtime cocktail for myself. I put *South Pacific* on the victrola, my feet up on the desk, and all thoughts of Uptown Judy in abeyance. I considered briefly Ratso's offer for me to write an article for *High Times* magazine, a popular drug and paraphernalia publication of which Ratso was a former editor. *High Times* often featured a pull-out center-fold section devoted to high-fashion photographs of high-quality cocaine. It was never clear how widely read the mag was but a lot of people liked to try to snort the centerfold.

Ratso had made two suggestions for the subject matter of the proposed article. One was a piece about my Peace Corps experiences in the jungles of Borneo. The other was a piece about my almost total repression of my experiences with Uptown Judy. In either case, Ratso had suggested that the title of the article should be: 'My Scrotum Flew Tourist – A Personal Odyssey.'

I had my doubts.

I patted the pizza box a few times affectionately, killed the lights, and headed off to bed at an obscenely early hour. The week ahead promised to be a very busy and productive one. A still, small voice within was beginning to whisper to me. This had occurred before, and it was always a harbinger of the solution of a case being just within my grasp. The possibility existed, of course, that it could just be gas. But something about the voice caused me to do what my mother always believed I could: Listen with my heart. Something about the voice told me that when I solved the case, and I had no doubt now that I would, it would always remain, in some very significant ways, spiritually insoluble.

Because of these inner circumstances, I very briefly considered a bedtime prayer. Then I said to hell with it. Let the good Christians around the world pray for my eternal soul. Let the little old man with a beanie traverse the slums of South America and tell the hopeless, starving, uneducated families of twelve not to use rubbers. It cost forty million dollars for him to make the trip. Why couldn't the Catholic church spend it on feeding all the cats left behind by all the witches of the world that it had burned?

The cat and I were about halfway to Sandland when the phones began ringing violently. We both leaped sideways and I collared the little slightly effeminate princess bedside blower that remained from a former occupant. Probably the guy in the floral kimono at Uptown Judy's place. Judy herself, of course, seemed now almost certainly to be on perpetual call forward.

'Let's have it,' I said into the ridiculous little pink speaker.

'Kinky!' screamed Downtown Judy. 'Kinky!' She was clearly hysterical.

'Hold the weddin',' I said. 'Tell me what's happened.'

'It's Mick,' she said. 'Mick Brennan's been burned to death!'

33

It wasn't far from Sandland to hell, but the ride over in the hack seemed interminable. The driver, a gaunt woman, who vaguely resembled a witch to the superstitious mind, managed to catch every pothole and every red light. The potholes didn't bother me but each red light seemed to be taking the gestation period of an elephant off my life. For a brief fantastic moment I wished I were Dumbo the Elephant. With my big, floppy-disc ears I would fly like the Kayan witches of Borneo, collect Jiminy Cricket or that tedious circus mouse somewhere along the way, and arrive in time to save Mick Brennan with the coffee-colored water from the Baram River in my trunk. I blew my nose in a black bandanna. I didn't know what it meant in the homosexual color code but it hardly seemed to matter at the moment.

'C'mon,' I shouted to the driver, after waiting several years at a red light. 'It's an emergency.'

'Okay, it's an emergency,' she said. 'Where's the fire?'

As we pulled over to the address on Canal Street we saw it. It was a five-story warehouse type building and fire was engulfing the top floor. The flames were painfully visible in the top floor windows like hellish heretical tongues licking lasciviously at the New York night.

With the sounds of sirens far in the distance I threw some money at the driver and ran to a small landing on the side of the building. The bottom floor looked cool and collected. No one around. There was an intercom and a row of rusty buttons that seemed like they belonged on the uniform of a soldier on the Russian Front. The names meant nothing to me. The door felt cold. I tried it for the hell of it. It opened big and slowly like a children's storybook.

I looked up and saw black smoke beginning to wreath the top of the building. The pope was dead, I thought. But I was not ready to give up on Mick Brennan.

'Mick!' I shouted. 'Judy!'

Nothing but the sirens getting closer, always, seemingly, infuriatingly, taking their time at times like this. I looked around for any sign of life on the planet. It was a dark corner of Canal and Nowhere and, of course, there was nothing. I entered slowly, carefully, as if the fiery building were a virgin. As I came to the first stairwell, it began vaguely dawning on me what the place probably was. The studio of the reputed snuff film photographer. That would make sense. Judy had called Brennan and they'd agreed to rendezvous here.

I ran up to the second floor, still seeing no signs of the

fire. In fact, there was no activity at all. Possibly, the bottom floors were warehouses or offices of some kind. At the third floor I began to hear crackling noises and things exploding above me. I still couldn't smell the smoke but my beezer was not the best after years of cigar-smoking, cat fur, and recreational drug use. I shouted for Mick and Judy again. Nothing.

On the fourth level I smelled the smoke and began hearing noises both above and below me. Downstairs, the rescue units were entering the building. Upstairs, I could only imagine. On the way up to the top floor I could see the smoke and feel the heat. On the landing at the top of the stairs a form was moving. Crouching to stay under a layer of smoke, I made my way carefully toward it. It was Downtown Judy.

Her face was smudged and she looked disoriented, and she wandered dazedly along the stairwell. 'Oh, God,' she said. 'Mick told me the guy's studio was up here and the guy definitely had the photos of Uptown Judy. He told me to wait outside and watch in case the guy came back. Then Mick went up and – I saw the fire – I heard him screaming – I tried to get through – '

'Stay right here,' I said.

I crawled under the smoke to the door of the guy's studio. I kicked at the door but it didn't budge. Behind it I could hear what hell must be like – rushing, hissing, cracking, swooshing sounds – the kind of noises most people usually only hear in their dreams. I banged on the door and burned my hand. I yelled repeatedly for Mick. I was still yelling his name when a hand grabbed me hard from the back. It was a guy from the fire department rescue unit.

'Let's rock 'n' roll,' he said.

Outside in the cold, Judy and I huddled in a blanket as

the rescue teams went to work. Her eyes had a glazed look and she was shivering.

'Where'd you call me from?' I said.

She didn't seem to hear my question. I asked her again.

'When I heard the screaming I ran up there. I couldn't get in the door and the wall was hot. I ran back down to the payphone around the corner and called 911. Then I called you. Then I – must've run back up to try to help Mick.'

'You did your best,' I said.

We waited for a long time while the crews brought men and equipment into the building. Somebody gave us some coffee.

'Is there any hope for someone up there?' I asked a fireman standing by a truck.

'There's always hope,' he said. 'I've seen 'em bring 'em out of places lots worse than this.'

Something collapsed upstairs. Sparks went shimmering up into the skyline. My guts seemed to turn inside me. There was hope all right. It was the 'thing with feathers that perches in the soul.' There was also death. It was the thing that disappears like little fireflies into the cold gray canopy of heaven.

Moments later, two rescue guys carried a large black canvas bag with a zipper all down the side of it. I'd seen those bags before. Most recently when they'd taken a guitar player named Tequila out of my rain room and left his face and half his brains behind in the rub. I didn't have to ask anybody if there was any hope now.

'Can I see the body?' I asked one of the guys carrying the bag. 'Maybe I can identify it.'

'Forget it,' he said. 'If you'd known this guy since he was a kid, you wouldn't know him now. Gonna take dental records, my man.'

Elvis, Jesus and Coca-Cola

I decided to take Judy and go over to McGovern's. I left his number with a guy from the rescue unit in case anything further transpired. Not that anyone expected anything. Once they've shown you the body bag it's pretty hard for them to Part II you.

After a cab ride that I hardly remember, we rang McGovern's buzzer about seven times and he finally let us in. He took one look at the two of us and knew it was bad. He didn't know how bad. He and Brennan had been close for a lot of years. Not enough to i.d. the contents of a body bag, but just about enough to break your heart.

I'll spare you the tragic details but a lot of Irish Whiskey got drunk in the next hour or two. I did a lot of pacing in front of McGovern's fireplace, McGovern sat in his old overstuffed chair staring at the fire, and Judy remembered a few more pieces of information, including the name of the snuff film photog that owned the studio. It was Dennis Malowitz. Not that this knowledge meant a damn to any of us anymore. I felt as drunk and numb as I'd ever been in my life and that was going a ways.

McGovern was still in the same position, Judy was sitting like a ragdoll in a chair by the little table, and I'd halfway passed out on the couch which had been to England and back on the QE2. Mick Brennan had made that trip across the ol' herring pond many times in his life, but he'd never make it again.

I was deciding whether to hang myself from McGovern's shower rod or wait a while and do it when I got to my place. Mick's death was as much my fault, I felt, as if I'd killed him with my own hands. I could let Stephanie DuPont take the cat. Of course, Clemmie and Daisy might not go for that. Maybe Winnie Katz'd take her again. I didn't have to tell her that this time it'd be forever. Maybe –.

The buzzer rang.

I started to get up but McGovern was already there pushing the voice button. For a large, drunken Irishman, he could move pretty fast.

'Mate,' we heard a voice say. 'Mate. It's Brennan. Let me in the fuckin' door.'

The three of us ran down the hallway and McGovern picked Brennan up about four feet off the floor in a giant bear hug. When we got Brennan into McGovern's apartment he didn't look any the worse for wear except for the sizable knot on his head. Apparently, he'd never gotten into the building at all. He'd left Judy at the rendezvous point nearby and somebody'd waylaid him on the side street off Canal. When he came to, the rescue unit gave him McGovern's number.

'Now where's the Bushmills?' said Brennan.

We hollered and celebrated and hugged Mick and jumped around for a while until the old lady downstairs began jabbing her ceiling rather violently with the broom.

'Fuck her,' said McGovern. 'Mick! I never thought I'd be this happy to see you.'

'You probably never will be again, mate,' said Brennan.

McGovern's loud Irish laughter filled the little apartment and shook the piles of old newspapers like a small earthquake. We had another round or two, and then, as dawn began surreptitiously slithering through the dusty Venetian blinds, Brennan turned to me quite seriously.

'Bit odd, isn't it, mate,' he said. 'They clear Uptown Judy's photos out of her flat. Now they knock me on the head and torch this bloke's studio.'

I toasted Brennan's health with a final shot of Black Bush for the road. I lit a cigar.

'Some people,' I said, 'don't like to have their pictures taken.'

34

'So this is sort of a secular Last Supper,' I said, 'for the Village Irregulars.'

'Oh,' said Chinga, 'can I be Judas?'

I ignored the comment. It was several days since the snuff film fire and I'd invited the whole group to Luna's Restaurant in Little Italy. Unlike Jesus, whose last words at the end of the meal reportedly were 'Separate checks', I was rather grudgingly happy to reward everybody for their hard work.

'We're here,' I said, 'to celebrate Mick Brennan's presence among us – '

'Cheers, mates,' said Brennan, holding up a glass of wine. 'I'd like to propose a toast to myself – '

'Who he?' said Ratso in his Sly Stone falsetto.

' – to celebrate Mick Brennan's presence among us,' I continued, 'which is already starting to get up my sleeve, and to inform you all that, while the search for Uptown Judy and for the mysterious person on the Elvis film (whom we will not mention because of our present locus) continues, we are asking the Village Irregulars to oblige us by taking a little sabbatical.'

'Who's we?' said Rambam. 'You got a mouse in your pocket?'

'Just the little ol' royal "we",' I said. 'I appreciate everything all of you have done.'

'He's solved the case,' said Ratso. 'I know you, Sherlock.'

'My dear Ratso,' I said, 'it is true that we've cleverly recovered the Elvis film for Tom Baker's father, but the case itself is far from solved. Some patterns, however, are beginning to emerge.'

'Some patterns,' said Ratso, 'are beginning to emerge in my *zuppa da pesce*.'

'Hey,' said Chinga, 'I just got aboard this ship and you're already puttin' it in mothballs.'

'Yeah,' I said, 'but it's a mighty big moth.'

Reactions among the group varied from relief to irritation to ennui. I tried to assure them that I was not permanently disbanding the Village Irregulars, just asking them to give it a rest.

'You want us to cut you some slack,' said Chinga, 'while you and Rambam solve the case.'

'Lighten up on the Kinkster,' said Downtown Judy. 'Whatever his methods are, they've worked in the past. He must have good reasons for doing what he's doing.'

'Right,' said Ratso. 'Let's celebrate. Let's order some champagne.'

'How about some Dom Perignon?' said Judy.

'That's *very* coochi-poochi-boomalini,' I said. 'I'll just have some more wine.'

'Yeah,' said McGovern, 'let's have some dago red.'

'Let's just watch our mouth,' said Rambam, as the large Italian waiter hovered near by.

Downtown Judy prevailed and ordered several bottles of Dom Perignon, which rapidly were poured down the throats of the Village Irregulars, some of whom were becoming not a little inebriated.

'What if we're just sittin' here,' said Brennan, 'and a guy comes in wearing strange old-country garb. You know an old felt hat and a coat that's several decades out of fashion.'

'Yeah?' said Rambam. 'What's your point?'

'The guy's kinda familiar-lookin', wearing this old funny hat and suddenly the room gets real quiet.'

'I don't like where this is going,' I said to McGovern.

'Nobody can control the little fucker,' said McGovern, as

Brennan filled his champagne glass with a maniacal expression on his face. 'That's why they call him the "Poison Dwarf".'

'I heard that,' said Brennan. 'But we'll let it pass, mate.'

'Christ,' said McGovern, 'that's a relief.'

'I wanta hear the story,' said Chinga.

'Don't worry,' said McGovern. 'You will.'

Somehow another bottle of Dom Perignon had gotten itself ordered and Brennan was already working on it. I hadn't brought my abacus with me but it was a good thing that the only currency I valued, in the words of the great Mahatma, was the 'coin of the spirit'. That was about all I was going to have left when we closed the place.

'There he is!' shouted Brennan. 'There's the bloke right there!'

The restaurant *had* gotten rather quiet. Standing in the doorway was just such a strange character as Brennan had earlier described.

'It's Don Sepulveda!' he shouted. 'Don! C'mon, mate! Join us! Have a drink!'

McGovern and Rambam had both made moves towards Brennan but it was too late. The man at the door looked at all of us as if he were marking our faces for an extremely unpleasant method of extinction. If ever a guy looked like a godfather, he was it. Of course, in Little Italy, any old fart dressed in odd, old-world garb can assume a demeanor, make a dramatic entrance into a place, and come off like a godfather. Nevertheless, the place, with the exception of Brennan, had gotten pretty damn quiet. Either the other patrons were stunned just like I was, or the guy *was* some kind of mob big shot.

'Nice hat,' said Brennan, in an only slightly more modulated voice.

McGovern was struggling with Brennan as the guy in

the doorway shrugged almost imperceptibly, walked through Luna's, and disappeared into a back room. I remembered Michael Bloomfield making fun of a guy's hat in Luna's once. Now he was dead.

'I tell you, mate,' Brennan was saying, 'he's a godfather impersonator.'

'You see what I mean,' said Rambam. 'You're an amateur and these are all just your assistant amateurs. This kind of shit is goddamn dangerous. How could you let them get involved in this?'

'I don't know,' I said. 'I must've had a nail in my head.'

35

'This has been unlike any case I've ever handled,' I said to the cat. 'We've turned up the missing Elvis film. We've learned that Don Sepulveda, contrary to popular opinion, is still alive. Maybe we should let it go at that.'

The cat said nothing. She stared at me with the gaze usually reserved for anyone insane enough to serve her anything other than tuna. The cat didn't give a damn about the personal or professional peccadillos of people. I didn't either.

It was later in the week and the cat and I were alone in the loft. I was smoking my JFK pipe, which now had a mildly aromatic flavour, no doubt as a result of residual cat vomit. In weeks to come people would quite possibly comment on the distinctive, somewhat exotic, aroma of the tobacco. No doubt, I would have to field many questions about what kind of tobacco it was and where I'd gotten it. I would, in that event, offer my guests a little port, tamp the tobacco a trifle, sit back in my chair and puff away rather complacently. Then I would tell them that a cat had vomited in my pipe. They would laugh. I would laugh. We'd laugh and laugh and garbage trucks would ponderously roll by, birds would sing in perfect quadraphonic stereo, little toy trains would derail, and people who really loved each other would go their separate ways in this cantilevered remedial world.

I had never particularly minded being alone and I minded it even less now that everybody was gone. I had the cat and JFK. Who else did I need? I thought of what Amelia Earhart once had told people who'd asked her how she felt flying so long alone in the cockpit, alone in the sky. 'I felt as if I were among friends,' Amelia had said.

Among friends, I thought? With friends like mine I didn't need a brown bandanna in my left hip pocket. My mind drifted back to the Last Supper scene several days ago at Luna's. I had almost forgotten it. Almost. Now I saw again clearly the strange old man in the strange old-world garb. He wasn't Don Sepulveda, of course. But he was somebody with a mystical, ancient, evil aura about him. Somebody you shouldn't say 'Nice hat' to.

Rambam may have been right. The case was far too dangerous to unnecessarily involve amateurs. Maybe that included me. Now that I thought about it, Uptown Judy had been one of the most mysterious women I'd ever known. Perhaps she'd always be. Maybe the very fact that I was having so much trouble getting her photo was significant in itself. Clap your hands if you believe in vampires.

I got up, made some hot chocolate, and paced around the loft a bit, sipping from a chipped, happy-face mug and puffing fitfully on JFK. The cat was sitting on her rocker busying herself scratching what, apparently, was an exceedingly troublesome flea. Every now and then she looked up at me with pity in her eyes.

'Something tells me,' I said, 'that one of the reasons this case hasn't been solved is that I don't really want to know.'

The cat said nothing.

That was fine with me.

36

The following afternoon, Downtown Judy, JFK, and I were sitting by my kitchen window. Two of us were smoking contentedly.

'That's nice-smelling tobacco,' she said. 'Has kind of a sweet, tangy smell to it. Where'd you get it?'

'Don't ask,' I said.

'Okay,' she said. 'Then let me ask you something else. How're you coming along on the Don Sepulveda case now that you've fired all the Village Irregulars?'

'I didn't fire the Village Irregulars. I just asked them to get a life while they were still breathing. There's already been so much death surrounding this case – Uptown Judy, Legs, Malowitz the snuff film king. About the only source of hope for our souls is the apparent resurrection of Don Sepulveda.'

'So you think you'll find him?'

'Secrets like this, my dear, don't remain secrets very long. Too many people know already. There've been too many deaths for me not to follow it through. Don Sepulveda has very little chance now. If I don't find him, the killer or killers of Uptown Judy will. Other mob factions will. Possibly, even the police will. The net's already closing in around Sepulveda as it is around those who murdered Uptown Judy.'

Here, I paused dramatically to re-light my pipe. I paced
a bit with the pipe and found, as opposed to the cigar, it
seemed to lend an additional credence to my words.
Smelled good, too.

'Very soon now Rambam will be getting Uptown Judy's
photograph from DMV – that's Department of Motor
Vehicles to you – and McGovern will be running the pic
on the society page of the *Daily News*. That'll stir the
hunter's stew a little. I may even decide to call the Village
Irregulars out of retirement. But, in the meantime, let's just
sit tight and watch what happens.'

What happened next caused both of us to experience a
leap sideways situation. We heard a not-of-this-earth type
of keening coming at us from a point which appeared to
be about four inches outside the kitchen window. I looked
down into the few feeble rays of afternoon sunlight that
somehow had sandwiched their ways between the skyscrapers, warehouses, hammered metal, billboards, and
other crap that blotted out the sky and would've made it
hard even for Amelia to be alone. A giant of a man was
standing in the shadows of the sidewalk and gesticulating
violently toward us. It was McGovern, and, from his
demeanor, one would judge that he'd been there quite a
while. I opened the window and looked blandly outside.

'Whatever does he want?' I said.

'Throw down the fucking puppet head!' shouted McGovern. It was a little colder out there than I'd realized.

I went over to the top of the refrigerator where the little
Negro puppet head was forever smiling down on me like
a small, friendly Aztec god. I took the puppet head with
the key in its mouth and the parachute attached, and
hurled it out the window. I shut the window, turned,
and without looking back, continued my pacing.

'It won't be long now,' I said.

'Till you catch Don Sepulveda?' said Judy teasingly. She did not relish the idea of having finally been included in the Village Irregulars just to have them go on sabbatical when things were getting interesting.

'No,' I said. 'Till McGovern finishes off my Jameson's.'

Indeed, it wasn't long before McGovern entered the loft holding the puppet head. For some reason the two spheres, the puppet's head and McGovern's head, appeared like a child's display of the solar system. True to form, McGovern went right to my liquor cabinet and poured himself a stiff shot.

'What kind of bar you runnin' here?' said McGovern. 'At least you could have the consideration to purchase the makings of a Vodka McGovern.'

'We're short of help,' I said.

McGovern looked around at the loft with the cat asleep on the rocker, Downtown Judy sulking by the window, the dishes growing science experiments in the sink, and the evening shadows stretching all across the dusty floor like a German forest of death. Added to this was my own fairly obvious expression of irritation at having my solitude disturbed, and the truly tedious, almost unconscionable pounding coming down upon us at two second intervals like drumbeats of destruction from the Isle of Lesbos.

'When's happy hour?' said McGovern.

'Happy hour,' said Downtown Judy, 'is when the rest of us get a chance to get back on this case and all the action isn't confined to the Lone Ranger here. Or should I say, Don Quixote?'

'One don's as good as another,' I said.

'Well,' said McGovern, 'I think the Village Irregulars do add an element.'

'Unfortunately, it's plutonium,' I said. 'Look, you've all

been very helpful in the past. But these are extremely sensitive and potentially dangerous waters. There may soon be a time when everyone can share and care and help solve the goddamn thing together. Right now it's time for visions and revisions, thinking and re-thinking. This case is very strange and it's not responding very well to therapy. Particularly group therapy.'

'But two heads are better than one,' said McGovern, humorously holding the little smiling black puppet head next to his own, and smiling in an uncannily similar fashion. This provoked some laughter in Judy. It is possible that I might've even smiled.

'You're all my dear friends,' I said, 'but this case is also a personal thing for me. If I've made some false assumptions somewhere in the beginning, then we're all sailing off course, and we may encounter nightmare situations that would make the horrors of the Argonauts look like rubber ducks in a bathtub.'

'It's all Greek to me,' said McGovern.

'My word of honor as a furrier,' I said, 'as soon as I get a few things straightened out in my own mind, I'll let all of you in on it. It's just that things aren't adding up the way they should. I have to know what's going on in my own mind before I commit my troops to the field again.'

'You should commit Brennan to wig city,' said McGovern.

'There's nothing wrong with Brennan,' I said. 'There's nothing wrong with you, Judy, or with you, McGovern. It's just something I have to work out for myself. And I think I'll be able to do it. Fortunately, I carry my inventory between my ears.'

McGovern poured us all a shot at this point and we raised our glasses in a brief toast. 'To quote Tom Baker,' he said. ' "Use your head for something besides a hat rack." '

37

As the afternoon ratcheted down into evening, Rambam came over and, possibly sensing a boy's club ambience, Judy began making preparatory movements toward leaving. She made a phone call or two, looked around for her purse, then, as she was actually departing, walked past the red cowboy boots on the counter and stopped to admire them. In an almost enchanting way, the woman in her suddenly came to the surface and she forgot she was in a loft on Vandam Street and imagined for a moment she was looking into a fashionable window somewhere along Fifth Avenue. McGovern, Rambam, and I were suddenly passers-by on the sidewalk.

'Are these evidence or something?' she asked finally. 'I mean, can I try them on?'

'Why not?' I said. 'Everybody else has. Including Ratso.'

'Why does that not surprise me?' said Rambam.

As Judy took the boots over to the sofa to try them on, I left Rambam and McGovern to entertain themselves momentarily, walked over to the desk, and set JFK down to rest in an ashtray that had been cast in the shape of the state of Texas. Fitting resting place. JFK was only an airport now, but there'd been a time when he'd been an inspiration to many Americans and one of them had been me. I wouldn't have joined the Peace Corps if it hadn't been for JFK. I wouldn't have lived for two years in the jungles of Borneo. Ratso wouldn't be encouraging me to write 'My Scrotum Flew Tourist – A Personal Odyssey.'

I lit a cigar.

I was just about wrapping up my revery when Judy came Texas two-stepping across the room. I took a few patient puffs on the cigar and watched the spectacle.

'Try one floor up,' I said.

'They fit!' she shouted, as she danced by the desk. 'They fit me perfectly!'

She danced around the counter and wound up the little impromptu number with a curtsy to Rambam. He looked at her with no sign of humanity in his eyes.

' "A drive-in Cinderella," ' I said, ' "in a Chevy named desire." Take the boots.'

'I couldn't,' said Judy hopefully.

'Take 'em,' I said. 'Somebody ought to get some use out of 'em. Just remember what Sergeant Cooperman always tells me: "Don't leave the city." '

'You mean there's someplace else to go besides New York?' said Rambam.

'There's a whole world out there, Rambam,' I said. 'It's not as perverse, jaded, crowded, dirty, sordid, or evil as New York, but, believe me, it's there.'

'Come on,' said Rambam, 'there's nothing out there and you know it.'

'There used to be a place once called Chicago,' said McGovern, as he fiddled with the Magnavox and landed on some old ballroom music. When McGovern listened to old-time ballroom music you could almost hear the silk gowns rustling across the floor of his brain.

As I walked Downtown Judy to the elevator, McGovern was lost in the land of was and Rambam was locked in a rather intense communication with his answering machine.

'The past and the present,' I remarked to Judy out in the hallway. 'Both may be tense. But the future looks bright. Like the great Sherlock, I can't tell you everything

I know or suspect, but I can say that I will have unraveled the parallel tales of the Sepulveda Family, father and daughter, very shortly now.'

'I wish I could help,' said Judy wistfully.

'You already have,' I said.

Just as Judy was entering the elevator I remembered to double-check the name and address of the custom boot manufacturer inside the cowboy boots. I got in with her and asked her to take one of them off. She tried and couldn't. When the cowboy boots fit really well they're hell to take off. Especially in a freight elevator.

After some pushing and pulling and twisting I got the bastard off, jotted down the pertinent information, and told Judy it could be an important lead and that I'd follow it up in the next day or two. I'd started to help her on with the boot just as the doors of the elevator opened to the lobby. With the red cowboy boot in one hand and Judy's foot in the other, my eyes locked with the Sapphic orbs of Winnie Katz, who'd evidently taken a brief break from her upstairs activities.

'Pretty kinky,' she said, as she entered and Judy hopped out of the elevator.

I handed her the boot through the open door. She shot me a quizzical look at Winnie.

'That's just Winnie,' I said, gesturing to the impatient feminine form on the far side of the otis box. 'She runs the wonderful alternative-lifestyle dance class in the loft above me. You may not've heard of it but you've certainly heard it.'

'It's not a dance class,' said Winnie evenly. 'It's a place where uninhibited women are not afraid to be who they are.'

'Don't forget that,' I said to Judy, and I winked just before the doors closed.

'Four, please,' I said to Winnie, who was obviously not in a position to reach the buttons which were only about two inches away from my right iris.

Winnie laughed a strange and knowing laugh, which, for some reason, made me feel uncomfortable. Then she said in a world-weary voice: 'Just push the buttons you know how to push.'

Einstein and Davy Crockett did not understand women, and there was no particular reason why I should either. No man really knew what went on between the earrings. You pushed the buttons you knew how to push. Winnie and I rode up in silence.

There was a time when Winnie'd been interested in me as her great heterosexual hope. I'd been interested in her, I suppose, if I were honest with myself, for the reason most men are fascinated with lesbians. To see if we have the social, spiritual, and sexual ability to wean them from their warped, wicked, womanizing ways. It fell a little short of being a noble aim. But love so often is driven by baser emotions, like a sleek, fast vehicle built with precision by remorseless Teutonic hands. Love would always be an expensive import in this world.

But all love aside, Winnie'd said something fairly cogent to the current state of affairs. She'd referred to her dance class as a 'place where uninhibited women are not afraid to be who they are.' Who were they anyway? And what the hell did they want? Not only was I fresh out of answers but it seemed that in the recent past a smattering of knowledge in this department might've been crucial to my understanding of a number of things. One of them was what happened to Uptown Judy. The elevator doors opened at my floor.

'Nice ride, elevator boy,' said Winnie.

I walked out and turned to look at her before the doors

143

closed. There was something almost poignant in her mockery. There were aspects of life that would always elude the woman in her that wanted to be a man.

'You've come a long way, baby,' I said. 'But you still can't write your name in the snow.'

I entered the loft to find a rather surrealistic situation in progress. Before I'd even said a word, Rambam was holding his finger to his lips apparently imploring me to put a sock on my vocal mike. With his other hand he was scribbling furiously on a piece of paper. The Magnavox speaker was not pouring forth old-time ballroom music from the FM station on the far right of the dial. Instead, McGovern's own rich Irish baritone was emanating from the speaker. Either McGovern was a very highly accomplished ventriloquist or I was riding a hell of a cat vomit high. McGovern himself looked like he was about ready to fall down and suck the carpet.

'Jesus, Joseph, and Mary!' McGovern and the Magnavox said simultaneously. 'What in the fuck is going on?'

It was a fair question.

As McGovern and the Magnavox rambled on in tandem, Rambam shoved the note he'd written under my beezer. It read: DON'T SAY A FUCKIN' WORD! THE PLACE IS *BUGGED*! IF YOU SPEAK, MAKE IT DIS-INFORMATION. REPEAT. DIS-INFORMATION!

I wondered briefly if Rambam perhaps had been watching a few too many foreign intrigue movies lately, but something very out of the ordinary was definitely going on so I followed the written directive. Not only did I not say a word, but, in addition, I put my finger to my own lips so the cat could see. While I was conducting this secret operation, Rambam was showing the note to McGovern, who appeared to be quite relieved.

A flood of thoughts went through my head now and

none of them were very pleasant. It's hard to think of situations and conversations retroactively and God only knew how long the bug had been there. And who in hell could've planted it? The mob? The feds? It all seemed like a crazy charade but the longer we stood there and listened to our hair grow, the less light-hearted the bizarre tableau appeared.

Rambam came over and whispered in my ear something to the effect that if a bug were an amateur operation, it could sometimes be detected through the FM frequency of a radio. This made about as much sense as anything else that had happened lately. I sat down at my desk, lit a cigar, and watched Rambam begin to case the room, checking the obvious places, under tables, the counter, the window sills. Occasionally, he'd whistle a bit in different directions. McGovern was watching Rambam, too. Then I saw him pour himself a stout shot and read the contents of the note again.

The silence was deafening. I got up and had another round with McGovern. When I got back to my chair I saw him re-reading the note as if it were a vital cipher that required enormous de-coding capabilities to understand. I sat in my chair for a while puffing the cigar in silence. Even the place where uninhibited women were not afraid to be who they were was silent. Then I heard the Magnavox and McGovern speak in loud clear tones together.

They said: 'The invasion will *not* take place at Normandy.'

38

The following morning I was slurping some *wonton mein* soup at Big Wong's and listening to Ratso try to put another bug in my ear about Elvis's background and

Kinky Friedman

extremely personal affairs. While Ratso was running down a *megillah* bigger than Texas he was also hard at work masticating a large order of roast pork over scrambled eggs and rice. Not only was it a rather unpleasant visual experience, but Ratso's detailed, arcane information on Elvis seemed to be interminable. I felt like Howard Hughes when he reportedly watched the movie *Ice Station Zebra* 250 times in the months just before his death.

'Of course, you know Elvis's favorite meal,' said Ratso. Once he got started on something it was almost a clinical recall.

'The case has taken a dark and unexpected turn, Ratso,' I said. 'The life of Elvis is now quite a peripheral matter. As are the lives of Jesus, Hitler, and Bob Dylan.'

'Well,' said Ratso, 'his favorite meal was peanut butter and banana sandwiches fried in Crisco.'

' – As are our own lives,' I said despondently.

'On white bread,' said Ratso.

'There's a shocker.'

'Oh yeah,' said Ratso, 'and with every meal he only drank ice water.'

'Ever the health nut.'

'You also know the bedside library he had when he died?'

'Let me guess,' I said. 'Was it *Polish War Heroes, Jewish Business Ethics, Two Hundred Years of German Humor,* and *Black Yachtsmen I Have Known*?'

'Close,' said Ratso. 'He had a book on the Kennedy Assassination, a book on reincarnation, and the Physician's Desk Reference guide which tells the name and properties of every pill in the world.'

Except you, I thought to myself, possibly a little unkindly. To preserve my sanity, my mind went wandering back to the evening before as Ratso continued to ramble

146

on obliviously. Rambam, mostly through his whistling
technique, had finally located the bug and squashed it.
He'd found it inside the porcelain Sherlock Holmes head
on my desk.

'An inside job,' I'd remarked, somewhat humorously, at
the time.

'Anybody could've gotten in here and done it,' said
Rambam. 'People who plant illegal bugs almost always
have to break and enter to do their job. There's no security
here to speak of.'

'There's the cat,' I'd said.

'Fuck the cat,' Rambam had replied.

' – The fuckin' cat really had some weird hobbies,' Ratso
was saying. 'He used to like to watch teenage girls wrestle
in their white panties with their little tufts of pubic hair
curling out. He had 'em do it right on his bed while he
watched. He probably did more than watch, according to
my sources. Anyway, he used to send his wife Priscilla
out at four o'clock in the morning for polaroid film.'

'Pretty kinky,' I said, absently quoting Winnie Katz. I
thought of what Ronnie Hawkins once told me: 'When it
gets too kinky for the rest of the world it's gettin' just right
for me.'

If the bug had been an amateur job as Rambam had
implied, then that, one would think, ruled out the feds as
culprits. The only remotely logical explanation I could
think of was that somehow some faction of the mob had
placed the bug in the loft to learn what I knew about Don
Sepulveda. If they thought they were going to learn much,
they were mistaken. The more intriguing question was:
How did they even know he was alive? A possible cor-
ollary to that question was how long would *I* be alive with
mobsters sneaking into my loft and planting bugs inside

my Sherlock Holmes head? At least they hadn't taken any cigars.

' – very strong speculation that Elvis was Jewish,' Ratso was saying. 'When his grandmother on his mother's side was dying, she called the whole family to her bedside. Said she had a very important announcement to make. Something she'd never told a soul. So with all these god-fearing, southern Baptist crackers – including little Elvis – around her bedside, she says with her last words: "Ah'm a Jeeeeeeeewwww!" '

I looked around the little restaurant but none of our fellow diners seemed to be paying any attention to Ratso's story. Of course, almost none of them spoke English. But they did know Elvis. They probably had always suspected he was part Chinese.

'There also have been recurring rumours,' continued Ratso, relentless as a Gatling gun, 'about an Elvis bar mitzvah in some town in Mississippi. I haven't as yet been able to substantiate this.'

'Come now, my dear Ratso,' I said, 'this could be very important. But you must be more precise about the matter. There are three questions that absolutely must be answered before we can get to the bottom of this: Where exactly did the bar mitzvah take place? Who was the rabbi? And who was the caterer?'

'Joke about it if you want,' said Ratso, 'but you asked me to research Elvis's background and I did. Besides, I've always been fascinated with how an ancient religion like Judaism still has an effect and an influence on our modern world.'

'I appreciate your help,' I said. 'But there is one further thing I'd like you to do.'

'What's that?' said Ratso.

'Pass the roast pork,' I said.

39

That very night the hatchet fell and it wasn't just the waiter bringing me the check. Rambam and I were leaving Asti's on Twelfth Street, an Italian restaurant where the bottles behind the bar and the cash register become musical instruments, and everybody from the bartenders to the busboys sing opera. We had said goodbye to Augie, the owner of the place, and, as we stepped out into the unusually mild night air, I was still singing 'Stout-Hearted Men' with some fervor.

'Gives you sort of a warm feeling down your leg, doesn't it?' said Rambam to a well-dressed woman walking a chihuahua.

I continued singing the old Sigmund Romberg song that Augie and about 49 waiters had performed an ace-boon-coon version of several hours ago. It was now a question of which would stay with me longer, the song or the spicy garlic calamari. There was only a homeless man going through a large plastic garbage bag, the woman and the chihuahua, who had also stopped to inspect the garbage bag, and two blow-dried, polo-shirted types talking on a stairwell. I'd performed for worse crowds than this.

I sang:

Give me some men who are
stout-hearted men
Who will fight for the rights they
adore.
Start me with ten who are
stout-hearted men

149

And I'll soon give you ten
thousand more!

The audience was not really into it. Only the chihuahua,
whose name, upon inquiry from Rambam, was Coco Joe,
appeared to be a Romberg appreciator. Nevertheless, I
persevered. If I could reach one person out there, I considered myself a success.

Shoulder to shoulder and bolder
and bolder
We go as we march to the fore
When – stout-hearted men
Get together man to man.

I had paused to light a cigar and to think of the next
verse, when suddenly, out of the corner of my right eye, I
saw something flash by like a dragon-fly wing. Almost
instantaneously, I heard a sick crack and a bellow of pain
from Rambam. He fell back hard against the homeless
man and the garbage bag, clutching his right arm.

'You dickheads took Frankie Lasagna's name in vain,'
said a voice. It sounded cool, collected, business as usual,
totally void of any old-time mobster accent. It sounded
intelligent, almost what we like to call college-educated.
For some reason I found this a bit unnerving.

Then I saw the guy. He was advancing toward me,
fighting back a little smile. In his hands he held a Louisville
Slugger baseball bat, obviously the same one he'd just
taken Rambam downtown with. I found this a bit unnerving, too.

As old-fashioned and out of style as the human mind is
when compared to the computer, it is still, nonetheless,
very wiggy to consider just how many images,
impressions, and ideas can be rapidly processed through

that ancient archaic mortal circuitry when someone in dress slacks with little tassles on his shoes approaches you in a menacing fashion holding a Louisville Slugger. Rambam had told me some time ago about the 'new mafia'. Young guys who never said 'dese' or 'dose' and had no roots whatsoever to old country customs or values. The new guys looked like they'd be at home on anybody's lacrosse team. The only things they shared with the old-time mob characters were an unredeemably criminal mind, and the ability to enjoy with equal relish killing someone or eating a nice healthy non-fat frozen yoghurt. Viewed in this light, the little polo player on the guy's shirt looked positively evil.

One of the guys stood slightly up the street to run interference, and the guy with the baseball bat moved in on me and Rambam. As he came closer, the well-dressed woman stood in frozen horror and dropped the leash on the chihuahua. Coco Joe, like many small dogs with great hearts, knew no fear, and went right for the guy's tassels. The guy took a murderous golf swing at the little fellow and missed by less than an inch, putting him on the final green. This bought a little time. From the guy's methodical approach and his partner's almost bored attitude, it seemed as if time was not a problem to them. They'd stay until they got the job done. But it gave me a chance to scuttle backwards like a crab in black bean sauce. It also gave me a chance to yell for help at the blinking neon Asti's sign. Unfortunately, inside the place, a large roomful of people were singing:

Give me some men who are
stout-hearted men
Who will fight for the rights they adore
Start me with ten –

I could've used a few myself. I tried reasoning with the guy as he moved in but he wasn't buying any. His eyes looked like Little Orphan Annie's. With Coco Joe still snapping at his tassels, he took two vicious swipes at me and backed me into a narrow corner between a brick wall and an iron railing. He was young and athletic and taking pretty good cuts. I didn't know if he could hit a curve but there wasn't much doubt he'd take me out of the game if he got another swing.

The well-dressed woman was now screaming and I was the one frozen in horror. There was no place for me to go except right into the bat. I dimly recall Coco Joe biting at the guy's ankles, and the guy's sidekick shouting at him to 'finish it.' The homeless man, who was wearing the last Mondale-Ferraro T-shirt in the world, was watching the whole thing as if it were street theater. In a sense, it was.

The attacker drew the bat way back over his right shoulder. Then the homeless man and I watched it arc toward my head.

At the last moment, the little polo player pitched sideways onto the sidewalk along with the guy who was wearing it. The bat clattered into the gutter. Rambam, using only his left hand, had windmilled the guy with the garbage bag.

'Grab some bench, motherfucker!' yelled Rambam in a rage. I remember thinking how fortunate it was that there was always garbage on the streets of New York. Any place else, I'd be looking for my head.

The other guy was coming over to help his fallen partner but Rambam had by this time awkwardly extracted a gun from a chest holder with his left hand. He showed the gun and the guy bolted for Fifth Avenue. The other guy wasn't moving.

I picked up Coco Joe and brought him over to the lady,

who took him from me quickly and got the hell out of there. She didn't want to get involved. Maybe she was onto something.

'Coco Joe's a hero dog,' I called after her. She never looked back.

'First time I've ever liked a fuckin' chihuahua,' said Rambam, wincing with pain as he tried to move his arm.

'He spoke highly of you,' I said.

With me holding the baseball bat and Rambam holding his arm, we walked back into Asti's. Augie, correctly sensing something was amiss, rushed up to us. At that moment, an Ezio Pinhead impersonator got up onto the little stage and began singing:

Some enchanted evening
You may meet a stranger –

'What happened?' asked Augie, wringing his hands.
'We just met one,' I said.

40

Didn't see Steve Rambam for a while after that. Didn't even get to sign his cast. With him at least temporarily out of commission, and with most of the old gang either coming out of or going into a sort of cosmic perpetual snit, I had time to daydream again. And daydreaming, as most government analysts today agree, can be hazardous to your health. Of course, as most government analysts today also agree, so can everything else.

The only bit of business I had to do all day was check out the store where Uptown Judy had bought her red cowboy boots. On the face of it, it didn't seem like a very strong lead, but a little Joan of Arc sort of voice kept telling me this was going to be my lucky day. Not that you should ever actually *listen* to those kind of voices.

I was reading Mark Twain's *Pudd'nhead Wilson* to the cat when I came across a particularly appropriate passage.

' "If you pick up a starving dog," ' I read, ' "he will not bite you." '

The cat, sitting alertly on the desk, looked mildly interested. Thusly encouraged, I continued.

' "This is the principal difference," ' I quoted, ' "between a dog and a man." '

The cat kept waiting and looking at me as if there should be more.

' "This is the principal *difference*," ' I repeated, ' "between a *dog* and a *man*." '

The cat, unwilling, or unable to draw the distinction between the two, walked over to the side of the desk and began sniffing the bowl of the JFK pipe. In resignation, I took a cigar out of Sherlock Holmes's head and chewed on it thoughtfully in the manner of Lt Columbo. I closed *Pudd'nhead Wilson* and was placing it in a desk drawer when I heard the Joan of Arc voices again. As if guided by them, I reached a little further into the drawer and came up only with an old arabic shawl or *kaffiyeh* that had once belonged to a friend of mine. She'd sent it to me before she died. Under the *kaffiyeh* were some old photographs I hadn't even realized were there.

I put the *kaffiyeh* and the photographs on the desk, walked over to the kitchen, caressed the espresso machine until it purred. The loft, I reflected, was turning into a halfway house for relics of dead friends. The red cowboy boots had finally walked out with Downtown Judy, but the *kaffiyeh* was still loitering around, and I had yet to remove Baker's Elvis film from the pizza box to have it copied for his dad. There were a number of other items in the loft that spoke of death as well. Too bad garbage sales were against my religion.

Sometime later I was sitting at the desk, sipping an espresso, flipping through the old photographs, sifting the cold ashes of my youth. I picked up an old photo Kacey had once given me. She was a child of about seven or eight, holding her father's hand at some beautiful, forgotten, faraway airport. The father, affectionately known as Jake the Snake, was wearing a dapper hat and trench coat and you could see he loved his daughter and she loved him. He had been a good-looking gambling man when the picture was taken, but by the time I finally met him life had put him in a wheelchair and me in a bad mood.

Kacey's eyes were shimmering roulette wheels of childhood, spinning stars into my soul, making me imagine that the child knew she was destined to die young and to frolic forever in the airport waiting lounge I was pleased to call my mind. And in her eyes I saw every woman I'd ever loved.

I no longer had to wait for Brennan or Rambam to track down Uptown Judy's photo or anything else. In a very real sense, I already held the answer in my hands. It was incredible, but it was the only one that fit.

Nice ride, elevator boy.

41

I took a long walk to Amado's Shoe Shop on Eighth Avenue in the thirties. Well before I got there I felt like an Adlai Stevenson impersonator in the wheel department. I figured I might as well have my own wheels fixed while I checked on the purchase of Uptown Judy's boots. As I walked, the sad, undecaffeinated truth kept stepping up and slapping me in the face. I'd been had very bad. Been looking at things through the wrong end of a telescope and they seemed very far away when, in truth, they were close enough for slow dancing in the make-believe ballroom of McGovern's brain. Things had been right under my nose, so to speak. Unfortunately, I'd already snorted most of the flowers before I'd had a chance to stop and smell them.

The cat was unable or unwilling to draw any real distinctions between a dog and a man. Both were large, potentially dangerous, not too bright. I had been unable or unwilling to draw distinctions, thanks largely to a cocaine snowstorm at the base of my brain, between a woman and women. Of course, I couldn't remember Uptown Judy very clearly. When things die they fade in reality and in memory. Besides, Uptown Judy hadn't wanted me to remember her too clearly.

But the chain of evidence was so strong that it almost physically dragged against me as I walked. I felt like Hercule Poirot, who, when he finally solves a difficult mystery, invariably condemns himself in rather brutal fashion for not solving it sooner. 'What a stupid oxen have I been!' 'I am like the blind man tapping with the cane!' 'I am the fool!' 'How could I not have seen?' 'I am the idiot!' Easy pal, I thought. Move it on over, Inspector Poirot. There's an old dog movin' in.

By the time I got to the shoe store, the chain of evidence seemed to be irrefutable. I walked slowly like an overzealous Christian wearing a giant cross heavy enough to drown a Budweiser Clydesdale. It was no longer that crucial what I'd find or rather, not find, at Amado's. But nonetheless, I had to follow out the lead. I had to be absolutely certain. Even when you're wrong, it's good to be certain.

The place was pretty much of a one-man operation, which was good, because I was becoming pretty much of a one-man operation myself. When I asked Amado about sales records for the past year or two he didn't look very happy. I wasn't very happy either. I could get along with this man.

'The record was stolen,' he said. 'By a customer. When my back was turned.'

'Same here,' I said.

'Happened yesterday. Don't know which customer.'

'I didn't know my customer either,' I said.

There wasn't a hell of a lot to do while I waited for Amado to repair my boots. There never is. I could've made the next move myself in this chance-ridden chess game of life, but something was holding me back. I took out a cigar, lopped the butt off, and fired it up with my phlegm-colored Bic. I puffed on the cigar and wondered what was holding me back. It might've been weakness. It might've been compassion. It depended on who was throwing the stone.

Sometime later I corraled a hack and rode it down to Canal Street. I got out at a corner where a familiar-looking building stood. The top floor appeared to be burned out, not unlike many people that I knew. I went to the corner and found the payphone, took a quarter out of my pocket, and realized the receiver'd been ripped off. There was rust on the metal at the point where it'd been severed. It didn't surprise me. Most payphones in the city were in the same condition. People here were animals. They'd steal Jesus if he wasn't nailed down.

It was dark when I got back to the loft. I knew what I had to do. I turned on the lights, fed the cat, and called the cops.

Cooperman was in.

I didn't really want to tell him what I had to tell him but I had to tell him. Or so I thought. But just as I'd resolved my moral dilemma in favor of handing Cooperman the solution, he wouldn't take it. He wouldn't even hear of it. The fickle finger of fate for once had pointed the way for me out of the labyrinth.

Cooperman, according to Cooperman, had successfully closed the case of Uptown Judy. Not only did he not want to hear my crazy theories, he insisted upon telling me his own. I threw on some spiritual bacon and let him rouse the whole barnyard.

'So we're supposed to be officially off the case,' said Cooperman, 'but really we're still kind of keepin' an eye on it. Follow me, Tex?'

'Like a detour sign,' I said.

'Don't get smart. Anyways, while you and your friends are out sharin' your feelings with Elvis impersonators, we put out a few feelers to a few wop operatives we know. They lead us to a guy used to work for Don Sepulveda before he got whacked. Ever hear of Frankie Lasagna?'

'Yeah,' I said. 'My grandmother used to cook him for dinner.'

'So anyways, about five years ago *babañia* started comin' in big time. You know what is *babañia*, Tex?'

'Is it a Hebrew word?'

'Heroin, Tex, heroin. Anyways, some of Sepulveda's people wanted to handle it and as best we can figure, Sepulveda himself didn't approve of it. So he got spliced and it wasn't nice. Never did find the body. So what do you think happens next?'

'Lasagna gets big in *babañia*?'

'You're a funny little Negro, Tex. That's why I like you so much. But that *is* what happened. And Lasagna starts to get well known and he don't need us but he'd like us to stay away from his action. So every once in a while he throws a little tip our way. So we put the word out through these wop operatives I believe I mentioned that we could use some help on this Uptown Judy thing. Word comes back he wants to talk and after exhaustive efforts on our part he tells us the word on the street is she was polished by the same soldier who is believed to have done her father.'

'Who was that soldier?'

'Nice young fella. Hit man. Worked for another family. Name of Sally Lorello.'

I couldn't believe what I was hearing. I fished a fresh Cuban cigar out of Sherlock's head.

'Sounds just like Inspector Lestrade,' I said to the head.

'What'd you say?'

'Sorry, I was talking to somebody else. I must've said "God!" ' God rhymed with Lestrade just about as well as Lasagna rhymed with *babañia*. Otherwise, there was nothing in Cooperman's whole case that made any sense at all when brought up against what I knew to be the truth. But if I had forever, I couldn't have proved it. Sometimes it takes longer than a life.

'You really believe Lorello killed Uptown Judy?' I said.

'I don't believe it,' said Cooperman. 'I *know* it. He's already confessed. He's implicated others in the Sepulveda rub-out. He's cooperating with the D.A. He's killed so many people he can't even remember all of 'em. He'll be going into a witness protection program.'

I sat there in sort of a shell-shocked silence, taking it all in. Even though he was wrong, Cooperman was obviously joined at the hip to his solution of the case and so were the official powers that be. It was convenient for them. It served a purpose. And besides, I thought, there was really very little innocence in this world left to protect. I looked across the desk at Sherlock. He looked back at me. 'It's just showbusiness,' said the head.

'You still there, Tex?' said Cooperman.

'More or less,' I said. 'What about Legs?'

'Separate deal. Like I told you. Probably drug-related.'

'Probably.'

'You still don't fuckin' get it, do you, Tex? This was an internal mob thing. We got the guy. The books are closed. Everybody's happy.'

I looked at Sherlock's face. He did not look happy.

'One more thing,' said Cooperman, making a displeasing sound that I came to realize was chuckling. 'What made you think *Elvis* had anything to do with this?'

I took a puff on a cigar and sent a cool trail of blue smoke upward toward the now-silent Isle of Lesbos. It moved gracefully in the air in slow motion smoke somersaults like the faraway fog rolling in on the Embarcadero.

'I don't know,' I said. 'I must've had a nail in my head.'

42

I went to bed feeling like the kind of middle-aged person young nerds always tell to get a life. I had a life. Unfortunately, it had been a fairly tedious life for some time now. Maybe I could recycle the goddamn thing, I thought, as I languidly counted Elvis impersonators to no avail. Perhaps next time around I'd be the cat in the court of the King. Let somebody else play the chess game to a stalemate. Let some other player find it too painful to make the next move. And what if the next move is wrong? What if Cooperman's right and the game is over and I just don't know it yet? I'd almost gotten to the point where I'd have preferred

Cooperman's solution to my own. It was wrong, but in the sad, empty eyes of the world, it would look cleaner.

Suddenly, Tom Baker in all his glory descended a celestial staircase and gave me a jaunty little left-handed salute and a smile that carried lightly across the lonely years of man. With that gesture and that smile, he banished all resignation, all despair, all sense of loss. I knew I was dreaming but I wasn't going to let it stop me now. I was on a roll.

Baker walked across to a small bar in a glittering ballroom, empty except for a skinny long-haired guy sitting on a barstool. The guy got up and hugged Baker like they were long-lost friends. They were. It was Jim Morrison. Lead singer of the Doors. He'd gone missing in action in Paris in 1971. It'd taken Baker over a decade to find him again but he finally had.

The two of them lifted their glasses in a toast. 'May the best of the past be the worst of the future,' said Baker. They drank. It was one of the two things they did the best together. The other was raise hell.

They sat there drinking, talking, laughing, catching up, for a long time and I could only seem to hear bits of the conversation. But I could tell they were very happy and at peace with themselves. It was more than we the living, even we the dreaming, could say.

I heard Morrison call Baker the 'greatest method drinker of all time', and I heard Baker tell Morrison it was incredible but he still looked 'like a hippie janitor'. Then they discussed for some length of time a particularly crazy notion. Baker had performed nude in a Warhol film, causing Hollywood to blacklist him from its pristine milieu. Jim had taken his johnson out for some fresh air during a concert in Florida, causing anybody that wasn't already upset with Baker to be upset with Morrison. I listened closer to be sure I heard them correctly.

I had.

They were talking about getting agents for their penises.

They closed the place together, stumbling out onto some star-lit, tree-lined California avenue, walking hand in hand like the last scene of *Breaker Morant*, into a grainy, black-and-white sunset. Tom Baker was home and I knew it. Even in the dream, or possibly, especially in the dream, I knew I was far from it. Maybe the cursed place didn't exist on this spinning ghost of a planet.

Jim Morrison had died before I'd even met Tom Baker. They'd been heroic friends locked in a fast-lane death dance in a rock-'n'-roll time beyond anybody's control. A piece of Tom had died when Jim Morrison died. But a piece of Tom still lived with me. Come tomorrow, I vowed, I would play that piece.

As Baker and Morrison disappeared through the doors of my perception, I traded a haunting dream for a ringing telephone. Not much of a deal but these days you take what you can get. I put a choke-hold on the blower by the bedside.

'Mit – Mit – Mit,' said a familiar voice.

'McGovern,' I said. 'What time is it?'

'Five-thirty in the morning. Are you sitting down?'

'I'm *lying* down, for Christsake.'

'Well, I thought you'd want to hear this. It just came over the wire. Don Sepulveda's been killed again. Happened earlier tonight in Bay Ridge.'

'You're sure?'

'They found fifteen bulletholes in him. This time, even *he* knows he's dead.'

43

When I stumbled out of the loft that morning they were waiting for me in the hallway. If you wanted to be uncharitable you could say I was taken by surprise. If you wanted to give me the benefit of the doubt, you could say I'd known for some time it would happen. I just hadn't realized it would quite be *now*. Now is always a bit sudden, as General Custer remarked to the captain of the *Titanic*, when he passed by in the night on cloud eight and a half.

The mind of a murderer, even when the deed may almost be justified, moves at a killer pace. It is driven always by that fateful, pilled-to-the-gills trio of teamsters: desperation, paranoia, and necessity. The criminal mind makes the normal mind, if indeed, such an animal exists, appear rather slow out of the chute. And any mind can become a criminal mind. All you have to do is taste somebody else's blood.

'I was expecting you two to walk up here sooner or later,' I said.

There was no one in the hallway, of course. Just a pair of slightly scuffed red cowboy boots. Though they stood there mute, I knew they were speaking to me from their souls. I took them back inside and, for some reason, put them by my bed.

Maybe there was still time, I thought. There'd be lots of it around later to sit and wonder where it all had gone. I slipped into my hunting vest, put on my hat, and grabbed a few cigars out of Sherlock's head. If I'd taken a few other things from Sherlock's head, the story might not be ending this way.

I didn't own a gun but if I did, I probably wouldn't

have taken it. Unlike many god-fearing, wonderful Americans, I'd never had a love affair with guns. If somebody was determined to blow me away they damn sure better remember to bring their own. I headed out the door in a hurry.

I left the cat in charge.

Riding in the back of a hack in a hurry was beginning to seem commonplace to me. At least I didn't say 'follow that car'. The spiritual hallmark of this case, of course, had been that there was no car to follow. I was afraid there was no passenger either now. Just a shadow in a dream. Just a girl I used to know.

It was getting on to be a bright sunny morning when I stepped out of the hack at the address I'd given the driver. A downtown address. The building was Downtown Judy's.

I pushed the buzzer by her name until my finger got tired. Then I tried the others on the same floor. I got a few cranky replies, explained briefly what I wanted, and somebody let me in. Somebody always does.

It was a fifth-floor walk-up and I legged it all the way. Past a child crying, a young couple arguing, somebody cooking some kind of zingy Pakistani breakfast. I walked ever upward past the routine archaeological layers of life, toward what I expected would be the last known address of a murderer. That didn't bother me. There was very little left to forward anyway.

A girl was standing at the end of the hallway on the fifth floor. She was kind-looking, carried a frail sensuality about her, and also, she carried a cat, gently stroking its head. She repeated what she'd told me through the speaker downstairs.

'She left in a hurry late last night. Said she was going to the airport.'

'Say where she was going?'

'No.'

'Say when she's coming back?'

'No,' said the girl, as she stroked the furry little head soothingly. 'But she gave me her cat.'

There was a certain finality to that remark that made further questioning unnecessary. I tried the door to Judy's apartment and knocked a few times kind of like you'd kick the tires of a car you knew you weren't going to buy. The girl continued to watch me and look kind. Both of us knew Judy wasn't coming back.

I patted the cat a few times myself, told him – his name was Atticus – that I had a cat of my own, and said goodbye to the girl. Never did get her name. There are millions of girls and millions of cats in this world and sometimes I wonder if we ever really get to know any of them.

The phones were ringing when I walked back into the loft. It was Ratso, burning with determination to give me some newly discovered 'background material' on Elvis.

'It's a favorite recipe of the King's,' he said. 'It's called "Coca-Cola Salad".'

'Ratso,' I said bluntly, 'this strikes me as totally extraneous information having no bearing whatsoever on the case.'

'But Kinkstah! The recipe is killer bee. I made a batch myself. You really oughta try it. Now write this down in your big chief tablet.'

'Ratso,' I said, 'I already know more than I wish to know about Elvis. But, in the interest of spiritual trivia, such as the fact that Richard Nixon met his wife at a tap dancing class, I'll take down this recipe. Now spit it.'

I got out an imaginary pen and a piece of paper and feigned an effort at jotting down the recipe. It was the least I could do. Ratso had worked hard on the case. He just didn't realize that it was over.

'Okay,' he said. 'First, take a large package of black cherry-flavored jello.'

'I hate it already.'

'Now add one 15-ounce can of crushed pineapple. Got it?'

'Roger.'

'One cup seedless golden raisins.'

'Unpleasant.'

'One cup apple chopped.'

'Ratso, I'm begging you to stop talking.'

'One half cup pecans chopped.'

'Why don't you chop your own nuts off and throw 'em in there?'

'One half cup white grapes. Am I going too fast?'

'Do chickens have lips?'

'One 8-ounce package of cream cheese.'

'Maybe he *was* Jewish.'

'One king-size coke. *King*-size, get it? Now this is important. You put the coke in *last*. Then you stir.'

'Ratso, I'm begging you to hang up the phone.'

'Now you pour into an oiled mold and refrigerate for six hours.' I took out a cigar and began my pre-nuptial arrangements. For some reason my brain was beginning to feel like an oiled mold.

'Let me check my notes,' I said, as I gazed blandly down at the blank sheet of paper. It was still blank, of course. I found that to be mildly comforting. I lit the cigar. It doesn't cost anything to be kind to a sick friend, I thought.

'Serves six to eight,' said Ratso.

'Does that refer to the number of guests or to their ages?'

I still had a number of things to do today besides laying on the phone with Ratso like middle-aged housewives sharing recipes. I was definitely red-lining in the humoring-an-old-friend department.

'Okay,' said Ratso. 'That's it. Let's hear it back now.'

I looked again at the blank sheet of paper.

'Can't,' I said.

'Why not?' asked Ratso. I took a rather paternalistic puff on the cigar.

'Because you left out the most important ingredient.'

'What'd I leave out?'

'One half cup of the case is solved,' I said.

44

It didn't take Ratso long to find his way over to Vandam Street. From the kitchen window I could hear him shouting and see him pointing to a newspaper he was holding. He looked like an extremely well-fed adult David Copperfield. I went and fetched the puppet head from the top of the refrigerator, opened the window, and tossed it to the figure standing on the sunny sidewalk. The shouting ceased. I closed the window, walked over to my desk, and waited. In his own way, Ratso had worked hard on the case, and he deserved to hear the truth. I planned to give it to him whether he wanted to hear it or not. That was the trouble with truth, unfortunately. The supply always exceeded the demand.

Yet even in the rare circumstance where the truth was sought, the truth-teller invariably found himself or herself subjected to ridicule, scorn, crucifixion, burning at the stake, or having to give Ratso a rather long, laborious explanation. I thought of the old Turkish proverb: 'When you tell the truth, have one foot in the stirrup.'

Moments later, the puppet head was back on top of the refrigerator, the cat had quite ungraciously retired to the bedroom, and Ratso, also somewhat ungraciously, was pacing the room, parading the paper in front of me, and demanding an explanation.

'What's goin' on, Sherlock?' he shouted. ' "Police Catch Killer of Mobster's Daughter"? "Sergeant Mort Cooperman says Sally Lorello is the man we've been looking for?" '

'Don't believe everything you read in the papers,' I said.

I finally persuaded Ratso to let me have the newspaper. It was the *Daily News*. Not McGovern's by-line, I was gratified to note. But it was a front-page story and Cooperman, in typically modest, self-effacing fashion, was taking full credit for cracking the case. It bothered me less than I'd thought it would.

I looked to Sherlock Holmes for courage. I took a fresh cigar out of his head, fired it up, and searched his gray ceramic eyes for a clue. He'd uncovered the truth on any number of occasions, and the police, the press, and the public of his day had chosen to ignore it. Now he just smoked his old pipe and looked at me. I smoked my cigar and looked at him.

'What're you and that porcelain head gonna do?' said Ratso. 'Sit there and smoke all day?'

'Ah, my dear Ratso,' I said, 'but smoke is all Cooperman's case is. It's a good solution. A convenient solution. But it's not what happened.' Ratso sat down heavily on the chair by the desk.

'So why don't you tell me, Sherlock,' he said. 'And I'm talkin' to *you*. Not the head on the desk that's never held anything but a bug and a bunch of cigars.'

'All right,' I said. 'You want to know what really happened to Uptown Judy? I'll tell you. She wasn't killed by some mob hitman named Sally Lorello. What happened to her was a lot weirder than that.'

I got up and went to the counter. I poured a stout shot of Jameson's into the bull horn. I offered Ratso a shot but he shook his head, kept looking at me for answers. I killed the shot. Then I gave him what he was looking for.

'There's a string of clues in this case,' I said, 'that stand out like a gaudy neon necklace of winking motel signs along an interstate that all of us seem to have traveled by too quickly. Nobody saw them for what they were, and nobody, especially me, put them together until it was too late. I'll bumper-sticker them for you quickly because if I stopped and thought about all the clues and signs and suggestive occurrences too long it would make me viscerally ill.'

Ratso took a sandwich out of a bag he'd brought with him and began setting it out on the desk like a little one-man picnic.

'Got any salt?' he said.

I brought him the salt in an antique Aunt Jemima shaker just as the cat came out of the bedroom and took a ringside seat on her rocker. I waited for Ratso to almost ritually salt the sandwich and for the cat to scratch a flea. Then, with all eyes upon me, I began what, even to myself, seemed an incredible narrative.

'First of all,' I said, 'let's remember that her background is very significant.'

'Uptown Judy's,' said Ratso.

'No. Downtown Judy's. And the fact that she was having her period was very suggestive.'

'Downtown Judy?'

'No. Uptown Judy.'

I lit a cigar and started slowly pacing. The cat and Ratso followed my progress across the floor with their eyes, Ratso moving the sandwich as necessary.

'She seemed a bit too strivey. Always popping up into my life at unexpected moments.'

'That's Downtown Judy.'

'No. Uptown Judy. And then, of course, although it's rather obvious, the boots did fit her perfectly.'

'That's Uptown Judy.'

'No. Downtown Judy.'

Ratso looked confused. The cat looked bored. I looked out the kitchen window at a line of dark storm clouds advancing on the city like Greek ships closing in on Troy.

'I can understand your confusion,' I said to Ratso. 'I thought I knew both of them but I was wrong. Now, to paraphrase Henny Youngman, take Uptown Judy. The times I was with her I was always cookin' on another planet. Why was that? It was almost like she knew. Then her father, Don Sepulveda, fakes his own death five years ago. That's an important precedent. Then there's the blood that Cooperman found on the floor of her apartment the same night Downtown Judy only wanted to cuddle because she was having her period.

'Then there was the phone call to Tom Baker's father from a woman who claimed to be with the Joe Franklin Show. She said the film had been stolen. Wanted to know if he had another copy. But the Joe Franklin Show received the film from Legs. How would they know to call Tom Baker's father?

'Then there was Downtown Judy's stunned reaction to the man doing the *lambada* on stage at Fort Dicks.'

'Don't remind me,' said Ratso.

'Yes, my dear Ratso, but I now believe it was not the

man dancing in his codpiece that shocked her. It was the picture on the screen of Don Sepulveda.

'Now I have no doubt that it was some mob stunt to put the bug in the loft. Probably they thought we knew more about Don Sepulveda than we did. But, by sheer chance, I happened to tell Downtown Judy about my plan to check the boot shop while the two of us were out in the hallway. Nobody but me and Downtown Judy knew I planned to run down that lead. Sure enough, somebody robbed the store of its sales receipts.

'No, my dear Ratso, we've been dealing with this case from the wrong mind set. If the boots fit, wear them. Downtown Judy was a very desperate person, a former actress, and the blood found on Uptown Judy's floor that fateful night was not Uptown Judy's. It was Downtown Judy's. And because she didn't want her body scarred so I would notice, I'm now quite sure it was menstrual blood. Deliberately planted menstrual blood.'

Ratso jumped up like a member of the House of Lords. 'Wait a minute! Wait a minute!' he cried.

I waited.

'You're telling me that Downtown Judy killed Uptown Judy?' he shouted.

'No, my dear Ratso,' I said. 'I'm telling you that Downtown Judy *was* Uptown Judy.'

45

A rare moment of silence was observed at 199B Vandam. For all the world Winnie Katz's lesbian dance class might've morphosed into a mime troupe. Ratso stood mute by the window looking very much like a statue.

'You stand like that much longer,' I said, 'a pigeon's going to shit on your hat.'

'But Sherlock,' he said finally, 'what was Judy's motive in all this?'

'Uptown Judy created Downtown Judy as sort of an escape hatch for her own life. She left my name at the scene of her supposed abduction to help draw me into the case in the hope that I might help lead her to her father. I theorize that the same mob forces that caused Don Sepulveda to do a bunk were also pressuring his daughter. Maybe they suspected he was alive but couldn't find him. Neither could she without a little help from her friends.

'After the don was whacked, for real, I mean, she could no longer afford to remain here in grave danger of being lamped by the feds, the mob, and, of course, yours truly. As I said, she invented Downtown Judy years ago. As a frustrated former actress, as well as a normal perverse human being, it became almost a game with her to flirt with me and to flaunt her theatrical talents. In fact, it was probably her best role. She certainly fooled me.'

'In the condition you were in, it wouldn't have required an Oscar-winning performance.'

'Sad but true. In my defense, though, with make-up, wigs, and various other nefarious techniques and disguises, creative women today can invent new identities almost at will. They are far more cunning than we are. As Ambrose Bierce said: "Here's to woman! Would that we could fall into her arms without falling into her hands."'

'But she's still a killer,' said Ratso. 'She killed Legs. She's probably the one who torched that snuff film character, too. And you're acting like her defense attorney.'

'Ah, my dear Ratso, but Legs was almost certainly blackmailing her with the threat of exposure of her dad, and she was protecting him at all costs. She was being a good daughter. She most likely did burn Malowitz's studio to keep us from obtaining damaging photographic evidence of her identity. She knew even I could figure it out if I could study her photos in a rational frame of mind. She lied when she told me she'd called from the outside pay-phone. It has no receiver. She probably called from Malowitz's phone before she torched the place. Anyway, he was a bad guy. No loss to the world. Maybe he was working in the darkroom and she didn't even know he was there.'

Ratso shook his head in dismay. 'Jesus Christ,' he said, 'I can't believe I'm hearing this.' He looked around dramatically for support but saw only the cat sitting on the rocker. She refused to meet his gaze.

'Listen, Ratso,' I said. 'Judy's gone now. She may be living in Quogue, Long Island for all we know under a totally new identity. New York is the world capital of anonymity. You want to lose yourself, you've come to the right place. And besides, I can't go to Cooperman or the press with this. Who'd ever believe me? I can't prove a damn bit of it.'

'But you could try.'

'I could. But there's something else.'

'You're soft on her.'

I took a puff or two on the cigar and glanced out the window. The dark clouds were over the city now, obliterating the sun.

'I admire her,' I said. 'Judy had nothing to do with Baker's death. And she had nothing to do with what kind of family she was born into. But she did what she felt she had to. In a strange way, I have a new-found respect for her.'

'You *let* her get away, Sherlock. You let your heart over-rule your head.'

'Hold the weddin',' I said. 'Did it occur to you that what

I've just told you is only a theory of mine. It does explain the facts, but it is only a theory. Downtown Judy may pop up nonchalantly in a few days. Tell us she's just been to visit her aunt in Hoboken.'

'Not Hoboken. Make it somewhere else.'

'St Penisberg, Florida. Lufkin, Texas. Who cares? The point is, Cooperman could conceivably be correct.'

'It'd be a first.'

All the theorizing had made Ratso and myself hungry, so we set forth to Chinatown in the rain. Cabs were scarce. By the time we got there we were wetter than wonton noodles. But there is something very soulful and uplifting about being in Chinatown in the rain. The sights and smells and sounds and neon signs all seem to run together.

As we walked up Canal Street toward Mott, discussing Nicaraguan politics and why I hated the Mets and Ratso loved them, both of us soaked to the skin, he returned to a familiar theme.

'Two things bother me,' he said.

'Me, too. The Mets and Nicaragua.'

'Seriously, Sherlock. How could you not realize, even in the pathetic shape you were in at the time, that the two women you were hosing were one and the same?'

'I don't know,' I said. 'I must've had a nail – '

'And don't give me that "I must've had a nail in my head" shit.'

'Ratso, to quote a few lines from an old song: "We come to see what we want to see" in this world. "We come to see, but we never come to know." '

Ratso thought it over for a block or two. Finally, he said: 'All right, I'll buy that. But why, if you think Cooperman is so dead wrong, are you letting the case go?'

'My dear Ratso, it's time for us to move on just like Downtown Judy may possibly have done. Leave behind old friends and relationships. Cut ourselves adrift from the excess luggage of life. We must go forward and poison new relationships.'

'You've had a lot of practice.'

'Ratso, there's a wise old Texas saying that applies to this case – '

'A wise old Texas saying is an oxymoron,' said Ratso.

Between the raindrops Ratso must've seen some transient expression briefly cross my face, for he suddenly softened his attitude.

'Sherlock, you look sad. Go ahead. Tell me the wise old Texas saying.'

I took a cigar out of the pocket of my overcoat but it was raining too hard to light it. I looked forward into the wet, shiny, neon-reflecting streets.

'Elvis lives,' I said.

46

One bright morning about two weeks later, a messenger arrived from Chinga's advertising agency, Chavin-Lambert, on lower Fifth Avenue. He brought with him a new copy of Tom Baker's Elvis impersonator documentary, Chinga having sent the original to Baker's father. Along with the copy was a nice new film container to keep it in. I looked over at the old, empty pizza carton still sitting on the edge of my desk like an empty funeral urn. I knew the comfort of closure would not be realized until I got rid of it. Yet I didn't want to just throw the empty carton into the trash.

Finally, I decided to burn the box right on the kitchen counter. Cremate it along with the Bakerman and Joan of Arc, and a sizable percentage of the population of

Hiroshima, who at least had been spared from watching Jerry Lewis do incessant Japanese impersonations in the years to follow.

I moved the pizza box from the desk to the counter and, mumbling a belated farewell to Tom, fired it up with my phlegm-colored Bic. Soon, two little bonfires glowed in the eyes of the cat. I poured two shots of Jameson's out on the counter. I drank one. Left the other for Elijah or the Bakerman, whoever came back first.

As I watched the pizza box burn down to primeval ash, I vaguely remembered something I'd read in the *National Enquirer*. They were interviewing someone from the Domino's Pizza delivery staff and he was discussing the trials and tribulations of the job. I poured and killed another shot of Jameson's to see if it might goose my retrieval system. It did.

' "The longer the driveway," ' I said to the cat, ' "the lower the tip." '

The cat looked at me as if I'd suggested we both grab violins and dance around the funeral pyre. But that was exactly what the pizza delivery guy had said, and, as mundane remarks often do, it applied to more than delivering the pizza. It was germane to the spiritual obstacle course I'd been through recently, and to the hell we've all been through and continue to go through in life itself.

The cat said nothing.
There was nothing left to say.

Later that morning I rang up Stephanie DuPont. It was agreed that if I refrained from licking her door frame until the weekend she would accompany me to dinner on Saturday night. This time, I suggested, we would both leave our animal companions at home.

As I walked over to the window I saw a small group of things with feathers perching on the outer sill. Some people called them pigeons. It was within the realm of possibility, I thought, if I could stop smoking cigars and Stephanie could stop referring to me as 'Fuckball', that one of them might soon take up a perch again in my soul. God knows there was room at the inn.

It was nudging Gary Cooper time when I heard a strange keening noise crescendoing upward from the side-walk below. I looked down and observed Ratso, my second favorite housepest. My first was everybody else.

The postman was arriving at almost the same time, so, instead of tossing down the puppet head, I shouted at Ratso to come in with the mailman and bring up the mail. Kill two birds and get stoned, I figured. Also save wear and tear on the puppet head.

Ratso was up to the task. Mere moments later, he entered the loft with an envelope and a question.

'What's a Vittorio Sepulveda?' he asked.

'That's Don Sepulveda,' I said. 'Judy's father. Recently deceased. Why?'

'Where's Valhalla Gardens? Sounds familiar.'

'It is. It's a bone orchard. Babe Ruth's buried there. You want to give me my letter?'

'It's not addressed to you.'

After a brief struggle I was able to procure the envelope from Ratso. It was indeed addressed to Vittorio Sepulveda, Valhalla Gardens, Valhalla, New York. My own name and address were in the upper left hand corner of the envelope.

'There's a pattern we've seen before in this case,' I said. 'My name appearing in places it shouldn't. But I was expecting something like this. You'll notice there's no postmark.'

Ratso grabbed the envelope and studied it carefully. I

took a cigar out of Sherlock's head and meticulously went through pre-ignition.

'It's an old Abbie Hoffman trick,' I said. 'No stamp. No postmark. Probably sent from JFK or somewhere. After a few weeks the post office eventually sends it back to the return address.'

'And you save the price of a stamp.'

'There's that. But also it doesn't reveal where you are when you sent it and it buys time before it reaches its destination. And, more importantly for us, the contents of this letter will most assuredly determine who was correct – Sgt Cooperman or myself. Ratso, the envelope please.'

As he forked it over to me, I struggled to keep my hands from trembling. Amazing, I thought, that it all came down to this. If nothing else, if I never went public with it or told another soul, it promised a kind of personal vindication that I now very much desired.

I opened the envelope.

I read the letter.

I smiled a crooked little moral victory smile. The way Hank Williams used to do. It was far from a perfect resolution of the story. And all compromise brings a certain sadness. The longer the driveway. If I'd been slightly off the mark in my judgment, at least I'd been correct in my basic assessment of human nature.

Ratso, observing my demeanor with interest, clutched the page from my hand. I let it go like a leaf in autumn.

'What the hell does this mean?' said Ratso. 'Some kind of code?'

'Yeah,' I said, 'but it's not the moral code some people are so fond of. It just tells me she's safe. She made it.'

I couldn't explain it to Ratso. The message consisted of only three little words, but sometimes that makes it easier to read between the lines. It told me that she was far away and almost certainly never coming back. That she was sorry for what she'd done but there'd been no other way. That it was useless to try to look for her. Useless to blame myself. That, this time, she was really starting a new life.

'We have another wise old saying in Texas, my dear Ratso.'

'And what would that be, Sherlock?'

'When the horse dies,' I said, 'get off.'

Later that night, long after Ratso had left, I read Judy's letter to the cat like a man in a mental hospital. Then I opened the desk drawer and took out Kacey's picture. Kacey would understand, I thought. Another little girl running away from herself.

I glanced around the corner at the red cowboy boots still standing beside the bed. They'd ridden their last rodeo. Sometimes it takes longer than a life.

In a sense, Judy got away with murder.

In a sense, Elvis lived.

In a sense, innocence.

I put Judy's letter and the picture back in the drawer together so Kacey could read it, too.

It wouldn't be hard.

All it said was: 'Elvis . . . Jesus . . . and Coca-Cola.'

Epilogue

On January 4, 1993, the cat in this book, and the books that preceded it, was put to sleep in Kerrville, Texas by Dr W. H. Hoegemeyer and myself. Cuddles was fourteen years old, a respectable age. She was as close to me as any human being I have ever known.

Cuddles and I spent many years together, both in New York, where I first found her as a little kitten on the streets of Chinatown, and later on the ranch in Texas. She was always with me, on the table, on the bed, by the fireplace, beside the typewriter, on top of my suitcase when I returned from a trip.

I dug Cuddles' grave with a silver spade, in the little garden by the stream behind the old green trailer where both of us lived in summertime. Her burial shroud was my old New York sweatshirt and in the grave with her is a can of tuna and a cigar.

A few days ago I received a sympathy note from Bill Hoegemeyer, the veterinarian. It opened with a verse by Irving Townsend: 'We who choose to surround ourselves with lives even more temporary than our own live within a fragile circle . . .'

Now, as I write this, on a gray winter day by the fireside, I can almost feel her light tread, moving from my head and my heart down through my fingertips to the keys of the typewriter. People may surprise you with unexpected kindness. Dogs have a depth of loyalty that often we seem unworthy of. But the love of a cat is a blessing, a privilege in this world.

They say when you die and go to heaven all the dogs and cats you've ever had in your life come running to meet you.

Until that day, rest in peace Cuddles.

Kinky Friedman
Medina, Texas

February 5, 1993